Critics hail Agatha Raisin and M. C. Beaton

"Every new Agatha Raisin escapade is a total joy."
—Ashley Jensen, star of the Agatha Raisin TV series

"Winning. . . . Cozy fans with a taste for the silly and the offbeat will be gratified. This long-running series shows no signs of losing steam." —*Publishers Weekly*

"Tourists are advised to watch their backs in the bucolic villages where M. C. Beaton sets her sly British mysteries . . . Outsiders always spell trouble for the societies Beaton observes with such cynical humor."
—*The New York Times Book Review*

"[Beaton's] imperfect heroine is an absolute gem!"
—*Publishers Weekly*

"Beaton's Agatha Raisin series just about defines the British cozy." —*Booklist*

"Anyone interested in . . . intelligent, amusing reading will want to make the acquaintance of Mrs. Agatha Raisin."
—*Atlanta Journal Constitution*

"Beaton has a winner in the irrepressible, romance-hungry Agatha." —*Chicago Sun-Times*

"Few things in life are more satisfying than to discover a brand-new Agatha Raisin mystery." —*Tampa Tribune*

Also by M. C. Beaton

AGATHA RAISIN

EDWARDIAN MYSTERY SERIES

M.C. Beaton

An Agatha Raisin Mystery

DOWN THE HATCH

with
R.W. Green

St. Martin's Paperbacks

Originally published in the United Kingdom by Constable Books.

This is a work of fiction. All of the characters, organizations, and events portrayed in this novel are either products of the author's imagination or are used fictitiously.

Published in the United States by St. Martin's Paperbacks, an imprint of St. Martin's Publishing Group

DOWN THE HATCH

For information, address St. Martin's Publishing Group, 120 Broadway, New York, NY 10271.

www.stmartins.com

Library of Congress Catalog Card Number: 2021029253

ISBN: 978-1-250-81615-3

Our books may be purchased in bulk for promotional, educational, or business use. Please contact your local bookseller or the Macmillan Corporate and Premium Sales Department at 1-800-221-7945, ext. 5442, or by email at MacmillanSpecialMarkets@macmillan.com.

Printed in the United States of America

Minotaur hardcover edition / published 2021
St. Martin's Paperbacks edition / September 2022

10 9 8 7 6 5 4 3 2 1

To Krystyna for all her
encouragement and support

Foreword

There is evil in the air and sinister intent when two people meet to plan the murder of a complete stranger. Most murders, as any police officer will tell you, are committed by a friend or relative of the victim, or at least someone the victim knew. Most murders also happen on the spur of the moment, in the heat of an argument, and in around one third of all murders in England, the perpetrator is under the influence of drugs or alcohol.

It is, therefore, particularly heinous for two people, both stone-cold sober, to sit down together and devise a callous scheme for the murder of another . . . unless, of course, the person with whom you are scheming is M. C. Beaton. Then, it's a lot of fun. That's not to say that M. C. Beaton—Marion—didn't take her murders seriously, but her infectious sense of humour was always difficult for her to suppress. Even when discussing the darkest moments of the most despicable crimes, there would usually be something to smile about.

When I first started working with Marion, she was recovering from an illness that made sitting at a keyboard putting her ideas into words utterly exhausting. Having known her for many years, it was a pleasure for me to be able to help, and I was amazed at how, having written scores of books over her forty years as a novelist, she was able to keep coming up with new ideas—new murders to test the formidable Agatha Raisin.

Marion encouraged me to chip in ideas, too, and we'd take the ones she liked the sound of, change them round a bit and mould them into something we could work with. Others she would dismiss out of hand as being "just too silly." She liked to have fun with the plot but she knew where she wanted to draw the line and needed me to understand that as well. The ideas generally manifested themselves as "scenes" in her head. These scenes weren't only murders but also included mishaps and pitfalls that she would inflict upon Agatha, then we would work forwards or backwards from that scene to weave it into the plot. I know it's not unusual for a writer to visualise how a story will unfold in this way. In fact, it's pretty much essential for writers to be able to "see" settings and events and to "hear" conversations in their heads, using their imagination to bring their characters to life. Working so much inside your own head is probably why so many authors describe writing as a solitary activity, yet every author needs someone—a friend, a loved one, an editor—who understands what they are writing and can give reassurance, encouragement and guidance.

Can you imagine how lucky I was having Marion to share my ideas with, and how fantastic it was for me to be able to absorb hers? In many ways, it was like being able to talk directly to Agatha. Marion put a lot of herself into Agatha, although any of her own character traits were exaggerated out of all proportion. Agatha says and does things that Marion never would have but may often have wanted to. This meant, of course, that Marion always knew how Agatha would react to a situation, because she was able to imagine how she would want to react herself. Marion knew everything there was to know about Agatha. One day, with the usual tea and biscuits laid out before us, the Rudyard Kipling poem "The Female of the Species" was mentioned and Marion was quite positive that Agatha knew all about it. "She knows her Kipling," was how she put it, "and she's also very keen on Agatha Christie."

That led to a very intriguing idea about which Marion became quite excited but, as happened with so many ideas that were veering off at an odd tangent, it was dismissed with a wave of her hand and the comment "It's good, but not for this book." That idea, that scene, then became another incident to be stored away for use in another Agatha Raisin adventure. Marion never liked to waste a good idea when she knew that there would always be an opportunity to put it to proper use. It became another moment in Agatha's future, another scene to weave into another plot. Marion, you see, had no intention of retiring, and no intention of ever letting Agatha retire, either. The inhabitants of Carsely, Mircester, Ancombe and Comfrey Magna, along with all of the other fictional and actual places in Agatha Raisin's Cotswolds, will never be allowed to sleep soundly in their beds. There will always be a murderer on the loose somewhere in the vicinity and Agatha Raisin will always be snooping around to track them down.

Sadly, Marion is now no longer with us. I miss my visits with her and the time we spent tossing ideas back and forth. She's still able to make me smile, though. Whenever Agatha faces up to some objectionable bloke like DCI Wilkes, I can hear Marion saying, "She's had enough. Now she tells him to . . ." and precisely what she tells him to do often has to be toned down quite a bit. So *Down the Hatch* has kept me, and I hope will keep you, in touch with M. C. Beaton through the inimitable Agatha Raisin and her wonderful cast of supporting characters. Never was laying plans for a murder more fun.

—R.W. Green, 2021

Chapter One

The scream stopped her in her tracks. It was sharp, shrill and chilling—quite the most horrendous noise that Agatha Raisin had heard since she had left her office for her lunchtime power walk. Summer was beginning to spread its rejuvenating light and verdant carpet over the Cotswolds, and Agatha was well aware that the season for strappy tops and floaty frocks was already upon her, yet she was not quite in summer trim. There were still a few stubborn pounds to lose before she could carry off the sleeveless red dress with the pinched waist, or the butterfly-print skirt, both of which she had bought a size too small as an incentive to lose her winter weight gain. With every passing year, it seemed this was becoming an ever more challenging battle to win. The navy-blue suit skirt she was wearing felt tight around her waist and a little too snug across her hips, even though she had persuaded herself when she dressed that morning that it would ease off during the course of the day.

Agatha sighed and looked over towards Mircester Park's children's play area. Was it from there that the scream had come? A small army of thin-limbed youngsters was swarming over climbing frames, dangling from bars, attempting to catapult each other off see-saws, darting from swings to roundabouts and from slides to something that looked like the bridge of a pirate ship. And they were screaming. Why did children scream like that? At their age, Agatha would have had to have a very good reason to run around screaming, or she would have been given a good reason in the shape of a clip round the ear. In a play park back then, if you fell over, you fell on concrete or tarmac. Grazed elbows and skinned knees were commonplace. The kids she was watching were careering about on some kind of rubberised, knee-and-elbow-friendly surface. Children were spoiled nowadays—cosseted, mollycoddled. Even a clip round the ear had been outlawed. Their lives were so much easier.

On the other hand, Agatha shrugged as the discussion swam around in her head, wasn't that just how it should be? Their lives *should* be easier. No one should use discipline as an excuse to beat children. Every parent should want a better life for their child than they had themselves. That was progress, wasn't it? Wasn't that how all parents should see things? Agatha decided that, never having had children, she wasn't really qualified to comment, even in her own head. She had never regretted not becoming a mother. She was pretty sure she would have been a good one—or was she too focused on her own needs, too obsessed with her own success, too selfish ever to devote enough time to a child or enough energy to being a caring parent? No, she decided, she had worked hard to leave behind her early life in a Birmingham tower block; she had forged a stellar career in London; she had built up a hugely successful PR business and then she had moved to the Cotswolds and established a well-respected private detective agency. Agatha Raisin could do anything she put her mind to, and had she chosen to become a mother—

The scream came again.

This time, there was no mistaking the direction. It had come from behind the tall hedge bordering the path along which Agatha was walking. She ran towards a black wrought-iron gate set in the hedge, thankful that she had changed her fragile office high heels for more robust low wedges before taking her walk. Bursting through the gate, she found herself in an area of flat open lawn. There were three people there, dressed in white. One was a grey-bearded man lying on the grass, one was an elderly lady collapsed in some distress and the third was an old man, tending to the woman. Agatha rushed over to the woman who was breathing heavily, clearly distressed, her eyelids fluttering.

"What happened?" Agatha asked, kneeling to talk to the man, who was cradling the woman in his arms.

"My wife collapsed," he explained, then nodded towards the figure lying on the grass, "when she saw him."

"I'll be fine . . ." the woman gasped, looking up at her husband. "A little thirsty . . ."

Agatha reached into her handbag and handed the woman a small plastic bottle of mineral water that was to have been part of her calorie-controlled lunch. She also grabbed her

3

phone, calling for an ambulance while heading towards the man spread-eagled on the grass.

"Yes, an ambulance, please. Mircester Park, at the . . ." she glanced up at a sign above the door of a neat pavilion that overlooked the lawn, "Mircester Crown Green Bowling Club. One woman collapsed and one man . . ." she looked down at the grey-bearded man on the ground, "looks dead."

Agatha stooped to feel for a pulse, first on the inside of the man's left wrist and then at his neck, just as her friend Bill Wong, a police officer, had once taught her to do. She held little hope of finding a pulse, and indeed there was none. The skin felt chilled and slightly damp, and one of her rings snagged on the beard when she lifted her fingers from his neck, causing the face to tilt in her direction. It was the face that had told her he was dead. The eyes stared up at her, cold, blue and lifeless. He had the bulbous, thread-veined purple nose of a man who was no stranger to alcohol. There was redness and blistering around his mouth and a trail of vomit running down through his beard into a fetid pool by the side of his head. His right arm was stretched towards a bottle of rum that lay just out of reach, as though it had slipped from his hand, and where the contents of the bottle had spilled out, the grass, immaculately smooth and green across the rest of the lawn, was scorched yellow. She freed her ring from the stringy beard hair and the head clomped back down on the grass.

A handful of other white-clad figures now appeared, drifting hesitantly across the grass like ghosts come to claim one of their own. There were gasps of horror and some quiet offers of help.

"No, stay back," Agatha ordered, "and don't touch him. He's been poisoned."

She stood to take a proper look around. She was standing on the large, almost impossibly flat grass square of a bowling green. It was surrounded by a shallow ditch that in turn was surrounded by a gravel path and, on three sides, the tall hedge that separated it from the rest of the park. On the fourth side, the gravel path widened in front of the pavilion which served as a clubhouse. It had a thatched roof, more reminiscent of Carsely, the village where Agatha lived, than the larger town of Mircester, but the thatch sat on walls of whitewashed brick rather than the mellow Cotswold stone of Agatha's cottage. To the left of the clubhouse was a small rose garden, and beyond it a substantial tool shed. Agatha gave a gentle nod of approval. Bathed in soft sunshine—and despite the whitewashed brick—the setting was quietly pleasant, tranquil. The current circumstances, however, were not. She turned back to the elderly couple.

"How are you feeling?" She crouched to talk to the old lady.

"I'm fine," she breathed weakly. "Please help me up. Charlie, you be careful of your bad back."

"Don't worry about me, sweetheart," said her husband. "You should stay where you are."

"Your husband's right. You shouldn't try to get up." Agatha gave her best attempt at a sympathetic smile, decided it was probably coming over more as a patronising pout and switched it off just as the sound of approaching sirens could be heard. "The paramedics will be here any second. Let them check you over. Did you know him?" She nodded towards the body on the grass.

"We knew him all right," the old man replied, "and we hated the sight of him. That's the Admiral—at least that's what he liked to be called—and I hope you never have the misfortune to meet such a foul, bullying loud-mouth. Loved the sound of his own voice, he did."

"Well." Agatha noted the venom in the man's voice. "He doesn't have much to say for himself any more, does he?"

A young police officer was first through the gate with a paramedic hot on his heels. The medic made for the Admiral until Agatha put him right.

"Don't waste your time with him! He's past any help you can give him. Get over here. This lady needs attention."

The police officer took one look at the corpse and, to Agatha's disdain, turned a very unattractive shade of pale green.

"Why don't you go and deal with those people?" She pointed towards the white-clad spectators. "Keep them back, ask them if they saw anything, that sort of thing."

Just then, the tall, slim figure of Detective Constable Alice Peters walked purposefully across the grass.

"Good afternoon, Mrs. Raisin." She surveyed the scene. "What's been going on here, then?"

"I've really no idea, Alice," Agatha admitted. "I heard that lady scream and rushed in here to find her in a swoon and a corpse on the bowling green."

"Okay, I'll take it from here." Alice bent over the dead man, feeling for a pulse. "Can you hang around for a while longer? We'll need a statement from you."

"Of course." Agatha watched Alice check on the old lady and talk to the young constable. She moved with an easy grace, and Agatha had to admit she was a very pretty young woman. She had long legs but generally wore loose-fitting dark trousers, which, Agatha surmised, were practical for the type of work she did but probably also helped to hide the fact that her legs were actually a bit on the skinny side. Although she wasn't as tall as Alice, Agatha prided herself on having long legs that were also pleasingly shapely. She caught sight of herself as a distant reflection in one of the clubhouse windows, turned sideways and sucked in her stomach. Yes, her legs were certainly her best feature, even if she didn't have quite the same athletic figure as Alice.

She peered at the gathering throng of onlookers, held back by yet more recently arrived police officers at the gate. The spectators were craning their necks to catch a glimpse of whatever was going on. She half hoped to see Bill Wong. Bill was a detective sergeant and the first person she had befriended when she had originally moved to the Cotswolds. His Chinese surname came from the fact that his father was originally from Hong Kong, although his mother was English and Bill had lived in or near Mircester all his life. Having outgrown the slightly podgy look he'd had when they first knew each other, he was now a very handsome young man—and engaged to Alice Peters. Was she jealous of Alice? Agatha mulled the question over for a moment and decided that she was, just a little. Even though she had to admit that Bill was a bit young for her; even though she might never have seriously considered a romance with him; even though Alice and Bill looked pretty much perfect together, she was still a teensy bit jealous. That, she decided, was a robustly healthy emotion for any woman, and it didn't stop her from liking Alice. She was a lovely girl and she seemed to make Bill very happy, which was really all that mattered, wasn't it?

Her ponderings were brought to an abrupt end by the sound of a grating, depressingly familiar male voice.

"Agatha Raisin! Always in the middle of it all whenever there's trouble." Detective Chief Inspector Wilkes strolled across the lawn. He was a tall man with an awkward, lanky frame draped in an ill-fitting off-the-peg suit; despite his undernourished appearance, unsightly rolls of jowly fat spilled over his shirt collar when he lowered his head to talk to Agatha. "I wouldn't have thought this was your sort of thing. No press, no TV cameras, no limelight for you to bask in."

"I wouldn't have thought this was something for you either, Wilkes—no pens to push, no beans to count, no backhanders on offer . . ."

"Be very careful, Mrs. Raisin." Wilkes wagged a warning finger at her. "I will not tolerate you slandering me in public."

"You need a manicure." Agatha took a step back from the rag-nailed finger, raising her eyebrows when Wilkes's nostrils flared angrily. "And you really should do something about that nose hair."

"This is all well below my pay grade," Wilkes seethed, "but I won't have my officers wasting time here when they are needed elsewhere, so don't try to turn this accident into one of your pathetic pantomimes!"

"Accident?" Agatha fixed him with her dark, bear-like eyes. "How do you know it was an accident?"

"Pah!" Wilkes waved his hand at the corpse and bent to pick up the bottle. "You'd have to be a fool not to see that this is just some old soak who drank himself to death."

Agatha recoiled from the smell from the Smuggler's Breath Dark Rum bottle, wrinkling her nose.

"And *you'd* have to be a fool not to see that this man's been poisoned. There's more than just rum in that bottle—and why are you handling it without gloves? You're supposed to treat every sudden death as a crime scene until you know otherwise."

"Don't try to tell me my job!"

"Well, somebody has to!"

"May I take that, please, sir?" Bill Wong stepped between Agatha and his boss, carefully grasping the very top of the bottle with his white-gloved fingers. "Forensics will want to take a look at it. Mrs. Raisin, Constable Peters is ready to take a statement from you now."

Neatly done, Bill, Agatha thought to herself, glowering at Wilkes before walking over to talk to Alice.

"Get this mess sorted out, Sergeant," was the last she heard from Wilkes. "Don't waste any more time here. I want you back on the Wellington Street burglaries."

Alice was looking over at Bill when Agatha joined her.

He smiled at them both before being buttonholed by Dr. Charles Bunbury, the pathologist. Agatha had once believed Dr. Bunbury to have the most interesting job imaginable, yet whenever she had spoken to him, he had managed to make it sound a humdrum mix of tedious procedure and interminable form-filling. Meeting him was about as interesting as finding an unopened pair of tights behind your dressing table. Although you know they're useful, it is undoubtedly one of the least exciting things that will happen to you that day, even if it's a particularly dull Wednesday. Agatha thought she saw a faintly forlorn look on Alice's face, and guessed that it had nothing to do with Dr. Bunbury.

"Seems like Bill's a busy man," she said.

"He rarely gets a break," Alice sighed. "We hardly see each other at all these days."

"That's not ideal, is it?" Agatha sensed there was more that Alice wanted to say. "Are you two okay?"

"Oh yes." Alice nodded, but then her lip trembled and tears welled in her eyes, to be quickly wiped away. "But he's moved out of his flat and back in with his parents. They insisted it would help him to save money before the wedding. Once we're married, they want me to move in too."

"For goodness' sake, don't go." Agatha shuddered, thinking of the Wongs' gaudily decorated house and immediately remembering the endemic smell of fried food that clung to everything in the place. "If you do, they may never let you out of their clutches."

"That's what I'm afraid of, and . . ." Alice gave herself a shake. "But this isn't the time or place. Can you tell me how you came to find the body?" She stood with her notebook at the ready.

Agatha rummaged in her handbag, retrieving a pen, and a business card on which she scribbled quickly before handing it over.

"Give me a call," she said. "I put my home number on the back. I'm not much of an agony aunt, but at the very least we can have a couple of drinks and bad-mouth men together."

"Thanks." Alice smiled. "I'd like that."

"I didn't actually find the body," Agatha began, "but I was walking through the park—I've been going for midday walks to help me stay trim—when I heard a horrible scream. At first I thought . . ."

After taking Agatha's statement, Alice left to follow the elderly couple to hospital. Agatha walked round the bowling green, taking everything in. She was no stranger to the sight of dead bodies, having become entangled in a number of murder cases, but there was something bizarre about the white-clad figure lying on the grass. She stopped at the clubhouse, where the handful of members who had arrived earlier were watching.

"Was it you what found the body, young lady?" asked one old man whose thick glasses made his eyes look like some strange kind of oyster. Agatha might normally have passed him by without even a nod or a smile, but "young lady" had won her over.

"Not me. The lady they took to the hospital and her husband found him. I rushed in when I heard her scream. It's a terrible business."

11

"Oh, terrible, yes, terrible an' no mistake." The old man shook his head and a gentle breeze lifted a few long wisps of white hair that were combed over his scalp.

"Did you know the dead man?"

"Of course. That were the Admiral. Everyone in the club knows the Admiral. Harry Nelson were his real name. Fine lad he were."

"Don't talk such rubbish, Stanley Partridge!" A woman with tightly permed white hair tinged a delicate shade of pink stood with her fists clenched in anger. "A drunken monster is what he were—an absolute monster!"

"Now, Marjorie, we mustn't talk ill of the dead," said Mr. Partridge softly.

"He were no monster. A tragedy, that's what this is." A small man with jet-black hair looking so suspiciously out of place perched above his ancient, wrinkled face that Agatha was immediately convinced it must be a wig joined in the debate. "The Admiral were the best thing that ever happened to this club!"

Several people now began talking at once, and seeing Dr. Bunbury saying goodbye to Bill Wong and preparing to leave, Agatha excused herself from the bowls group, hurrying over to her friend.

"So what's the verdict, Bill?"

"Ah, hello, Agatha." Bill grinned. "Sorry about DCI Wilkes. You two really know how to get under each other's skin, don't you?"

"He's an idiot. Our dead man was poisoned, wasn't he?"

"Dr. Bunbury was in no doubt about that," Bill admitted.

12

"He certainly drank something that did him no good. We'll know more after the post-mortem, and once we get the test results back on the contents of the bottle."

"Accident or suicide or . . ." Agatha raised an eyebrow.

"There's nothing to suggest he was murdered, if that's what you're getting at." Bill shrugged. "We'll talk to the people here and take a look at the premises to see if that sheds any light on what happened."

"But you can't rule out murder?" Agatha sounded a little too eager to hear the very worst news, and Bill felt too harassed to humour her.

"We can't rule out anything, Agatha, but it doesn't look like murder." He waved her away and headed towards the pavilion. "I don't know how many times I've said this in the past, but I'm saying it again now. You have to leave this to the police. You really mustn't get involved. Now if you'll excuse me, I have work to do. You've given your statement. If we need anything else from you, either Alice or I will be in touch."

"Bill, about Alice, I—"

"Not now, Agatha."

"Yes, we took the soil samples from the sites you marked on the map." Sir Charles Fraith leaned back in the leather chair, holding the phone in one hand and plucking his coffee cup from the desk with the other. "We'll have the analysis report back by the end of the week."

He sipped the coffee, silently cursing himself for allowing

it to go cold. He rested his head against the high back of the chair, his neatly combed hair looking boyishly fair against the dark, aged leather.

"Do we have to wait that long?" He placed the china cup back in its saucer. "Your mind will be elsewhere if you're riding. Can you make it for a flying visit this weekend? Good. I'll pick you up at the airport. Yes, of course, he would be most welcome to come. I'd be delighted to see him. Wonderful. I'll see you on Friday evening, then."

After a brief goodbye, he triumphantly plunged the phone back into its charger base and rang a small brass bell on his desk.

"GUSTAV!"

"You rang—and howled—Sir Charles?" Gustav made a point of using the white cloth he was holding to flick some dust from the shelf as though it caused him great offence before approaching Charles's desk.

Charles generally found Gustav's manner reassuringly amusing. A stranger might think him merely an impudent servant, but Gustav was far more than that. He had worked for Charles's father, and Charles had grown up with him as a constant presence in his life. Gustav liked to give the impression that he was a butler, but in the past, when money had been tight, he had been pressed into service as a plumber, electrician, cleaner and general handyman—the bedrock of Barfield House, the Fraith family seat. He still laundered, pressed and hung Charles's clothes, maintaining his employer as what Agatha Raisin had once described as

14

"a crumple-free zone." Of slim build, yet wiry and strong, Gustav had become integral to the character of Barfield.

"We will be having a couple of guests to stay this weekend," Charles informed him as Gustav retrieved the cup and saucer, tutting while wiping a couple of spots of coffee from the leather inlay on the antique oak desktop.

"Are we sure that's wise, sir?" Gustav clasped a hand to his chest and made wide eyes in mock theatrical horror. "The last time we had guests to stay was for the masked ball following your marriage—and that didn't end well, did it?"

"No, it did not." Charles's aged aunt, Mrs. Tassy, breezed into the room clad in a waft of chiffon so dark green it was almost black. A tall woman with slender limbs, she had lived at Barfield House as long as Charles could remember. She slotted a book she was carrying onto a bookshelf high above Gustav's head, perused a lower shelf and selected another slim volume. "You were arrested for the murder of your wife, Charles, remember? I'd like to say how much I miss the girl and her parents, but that would be a dreadful lie, so I won't bother. Might I have some tea, Gustav?"

"Yes, tea would be a good idea, Gustav." Charles looked at his aunt, shaking his head. "We really need to put that whole episode behind us, Aunt. We have to move forward. So, two rooms to be made ready for two guests this weekend, Gustav. A young lady and her uncle."

"Would that be the young French lady, sir?"

"Surely not the one who sent you packing, Charles?"

Mrs. Tassy sounded suddenly interested. "Immune to your charms? Quite a rarity. I shall look forward to meeting her."

"She did not send me packing," Charles insisted. "There was no romantic entanglement when I visited her in France—just business. She is coming here to advise about the possibility of establishing our own vineyard."

"*Très bien.*" Gustav headed for the kitchen. "Then the wine will not be tainted with bitterness."

"I hope he's going to be on his best behaviour this weekend," Charles sighed, watching Gustav leave the room and knowing full well he would be listening. "I want to make a good impression on these people."

Mrs. Tassy settled in a comfortably firm armchair by the French windows that overlooked the lawn and sat quietly for a few minutes, reading her book. "These people," she eventually piped up in her reedy warble, "or just the young lady?"

"I told you, there's nothing like that going on." Charles smiled. He was enormously fond of his aunt and very much aware that while she maintained a sternly old-fashioned attitude of disapproval when it came to his romantic liaisons, secretly she delighted in the intrigue of it all.

"I'd like to believe you, Charles, but I suspect you see this one simply as more of a challenge than some of the others, such as Mrs. Raisin, for example."

"Agatha is a very dear friend." Charles ran his hand through his hair, a sure sign, his aunt noted, that he was becoming irritated. "At least she was until . . . No, she *is* a very dear friend. I just need to mend a few bridges there. Now," he shuffled some papers on his desk, "do you intend taking your tea here? I have a great deal of work to get through."

"As I believe I have told you many times, Charles, this is the library, where one comes to read books. There are countless other rooms in the house you could use as an office. I have come in here to read, the purpose for which this room is intended. I shall be as quiet as a mouse. Far quieter than the mice that were stomping around behind the skirting in my room last night, at any rate."

"Yes, yes, so you keep saying. I'll have Gustav sort out something for the mice."

"I doubt mice are partial to Earl Grey," Gustav commented, returning with a tea tray. "Perhaps a Garibaldi?"

Harvey's only had three frozen lasagne ready meals left. Agatha scooped them all into her wire shopping basket. Carsely's village shop stocked an impressive range of fresh food for such a small establishment, but Agatha was the most enthusiastic and regular patron of their deep freeze. She added a couple of frozen shepherd's pies and caught a disapproving look from a woman in a pink woollen coat and a hat that looked like a sculpted blancmange. Agatha shrugged and moved on. It had been a long day and she was looking forward to getting home. She didn't need anyone criticising her. She enjoyed dining on deliciously well-prepared food when she ate out, but at home she had neither the patience nor the passion to spend time in her kitchen creating fantastic dishes.

In truth, she knew she was not the world's greatest cook. Not that she couldn't be if she really wanted, but in all honesty, she couldn't include culinary skill on a list of her virtues. Who could forget the year she invited all her staff to a sumptuous Christmas dinner at her cottage, then found the turkey was too big to fit in her oven? She'd used the big oven in the village hall instead, incinerating the turkey and almost burning down the hall along with it. She'd had to pay for the hall to be redecorated. Ironically, the incident had endeared her to the locals. Previously they had been less than friendly, almost hostile, towards her, but once the hall was repainted and every woman in the area heard of the Christmas dinner nightmare that so many of them had themselves come so close to in the past, Agatha was endowed with a degree of sympathy that, for a newcomer like herself, took her one step closer to being accepted as a Carsely villager.

Would she ever really belong? She pondered the point for the millionth time as, drawn by an artistically arranged pyramid of red-wine bottles, she crossed the shop floor to a row of rough wooden crates that had been pressed into service as rustic display shelves. She perused the wine while pondering her situation in Carsely. Even though her high-profile murder investigations had established her as one of the most recognisable residents of the village, did she really fit in here? Did she even care about fitting in any more? She had to admit that she did. She had chosen to live in Carsely and she wanted it to be her home. She *needed* it to feel like her home. In times past, she had often been so frustrated and disillusioned with rural life in the Cotswolds that she had felt like chucking it all in and scurrying back to London. She had even put her cottage up for sale. Nowadays she rarely felt like running away; she was determined to stay put, either with the blessing of the locals or in spite of them.

She found herself staring at a bottle of Primitivo, a wine from Puglia in Italy. She had visited the region on holiday many years ago and loved the time she'd spent touring the coast, taking in the sights, sampling the wine and trying out basic Italian in village cafés. She smiled, picking up a bottle to study the label. Would it have been any more difficult to fit in there than in Carsely? Of course it would, she told herself. Your Italian never progressed beyond reading aloud from a menu and calling to the waiter for "*Più Primitivo, per favore!*"

"A fine choice, Mrs. Raisin!" Margaret Bloxby, wife of Alf, the local vicar, was suddenly by Agatha's side, a shopping basket over her arm. Agatha immediately saw that she had picked up a cauliflower, carrots, onions and apples—a far more wholesome haul than her own.

"Mrs. Bloxby, how nice to see you!" Even though the two women had known each other for years, they maintained the quaint tradition, followed rigidly by the Carsely Ladies' Society, of never using each other's first names. Agatha watched the vicar's wife smile. They didn't always adhere quite so rigorously to the formality as the Ladies' Society did, but it amused them to do so in public. In private, especially over a glass of sherry, first names could sometimes slip out. "I didn't realise you were a fan of Italian wine."

"I learned a little about it when Alf swapped our church here in Carsely with another vicar on a foreign exchange trip. It was a wonderful experience."

"You were in Puglia?"

"Oh no, Mrs. Raisin. I shouldn't think there would be much call for a Church of England vicar there. We went to California, and an American vicar, Dwight I think his name was, came here. Alf and I took a wine-tasting trip in the Napa Valley, where they have Zinfandel, which is the same grape as Primitivo. The Italians even export Primitivo to the United States labelled as Zinfandel. I became quite partial to it."

"You are a font of knowledge, Mrs. Bloxby. Care to share some of this with me?" Agatha held up the bottle, then turned back to the display. "Maybe I should pick up another one."

As she turned, the corner of her basket clipped one of the display crates and its wooden side collapsed, turning the pyramid of wine bottles into a clinking avalanche. Agatha squeezed her eyes closed, waiting for the inevitable crescendo of shattering glass. It never came. The bottles tumbled onto the shop's forgiving wooden floorboards, rolling and clanking together without a single breakage. She tentatively opened her eyes to see an assistant hurrying over, assuring her that there was no harm done and that it was all his fault for having built such a rickety display. Agatha knew that Blancmange Hat and the three or four other customers would now be staring, but chose not to turn and glower at them. Instead, she stooped to retrieve a bottle of wine from the floor.

There was a sharp pop and a ripping sound. At first she thought she might have torn a muscle in her back. Then she realised it was much worse than that. She had torn something far more vital.

"Agatha," Mrs. Bloxby leaned in close to whisper, "your skirt has split down the seam at the back."

"Did they all get an eyeful?" Agatha muttered out of the corner of her mouth.

"A bit of racy lace." Mrs. Bloxby draped her raincoat over Agatha's shoulders. "Enough to keep them chattering for a week or two. My coat is long enough to restore your dignity."

"Thank you," Agatha breathed. "It's always good to have a friend covering your backside. Let's pay up and head for my place. I could use a glass of this wine."

"That sounds good to me." Mrs. Bloxby smiled. "I have to admit that I spotted you coming in here and followed you. You see, I have a small favour to ask . . ."

They made their way swiftly to Agatha's cottage in Lilac Lane, Mrs. Bloxby carrying their shopping and Agatha walking with arms folded, clutching the raincoat tightly closed.

Chapter Two

The following morning, Agatha arrived at the municipal car park in Mircester bright and early. She bagged her favourite spot behind a birch tree that had spread its silver limbs far enough to provide shade that stopped her car from becoming too hot and stuffy in the sunshine, yet not quite far enough to offer perched birds the chance to use her windscreen for target practice. She flipped down the sun visor, using the illuminated mirror to touch up her lipstick and smooth her sleek bob of brown hair. Then she stepped out of the car, backing past the rear door to check herself out in the driver's-side mirror. It was a well-tried ritual, but, considering the calamity in Harvey's the evening before, an essential safeguard.

Once straightened into place to eradicate any creases picked up on the short journey to work, she judged her grey skirt and jacket, the jacket trimmed with black silk around the lapels and pockets, to be sitting perfectly. The suit was lightweight French wool and far from new, although, Agatha mused, like herself it was managing to hide its age well. In any case, she reassured herself, it had classic lines, and class never went out of fashion. Not that anyone she might meet

22

that day would notice. This was downtown Mircester, after all, not Mayfair, Manhattan or the Avenue Montaigne.

High heels clicking smartly on the pavement, she made her way swiftly along the high street to where an ancient alleyway dipped down towards the King Charles pub, whose dark latticed windows looked out over the cobbles to a quaint little antiques shop, above which were the offices of Raisin Investigations. Agatha tiptoed across the cobbles to spare her heels, and herself, the indignity of becoming trapped in the crevices between the stones. Worn smooth by more than a century of rumbling cart wheels, iron-clad horse hooves, heavy truck tyres and the pounding of pedestrians, the cobbles were as slippery as oiled glass when it rained. She had taken to crossing them barefoot when they were wet, having once landed on her backside with such a thump that for the next week she had been forced to sit listing to the left.

Pausing to peruse the antiques shop window, she caught sight of her reflection, and realised that her right hand had drifted down to massage the site of the long-gone bruise. Then she spotted Mr. Tinkler, the antiques dealer, peering at her over his half-moon glasses from behind the sheltering arms of an oversized Spirit of Ecstasy statuette. She returned his bemused stare with a glower from her bear-like eyes, stuck out her tongue in a satisfying display of petulance and moved swiftly to the door leading up to her office.

At the top of the stairs, she walked into the main open-plan office area and nodded her approval on seeing that, early as she was, all her staff were already in the office. Toni looked up from her computer screen. Slim and blonde with dazzling blue eyes, she was in her early twenties and, Agatha reluctantly admitted to herself, was growing ever more beautiful as she left the gawkiness of her teenage years behind. She had the kind of smooth, pale skin that Agatha could only attempt to achieve nowadays with the painful aid of wax and tweezers. She winced at the thought of her last session in front of the bathroom mirror. Youth had no conception of such agonising indignity, yet age managed to keep the blissful memory of flawless young skin cruelly vivid.

"Morning, Agatha," Toni smiled. "I love that jacket. Is it new?"

"New-ish," was all Agatha offered. Toni was smart and pretty but she was still a Mircester girl at heart.

"Hi, boss." Simon gave Agatha one of his trademark grins as he stirred a mug of coffee. The grin wrinkled his thin features, making his pointed nose and chin seem even more cartoon-like than usual. To Agatha's eyes, he was a strange-looking young man. His dark blue suit jacket seemed too short, as did the trouser legs, which exposed bright orange socks above scuffed brown shoes that were as pointed as his chin. Despite his odd looks, Simon never seemed short of female admirers, and he had proven to be a valuable asset as a detective, even if his work could be a little slapdash at times. "What's all this about a body in the park?"

"Change the socks, Simon," she instructed. "Discretion is our watchword as detectives, and you'll never merge into a crowd wearing socks like that."

Simon's grin never wavered, giving Agatha the distinct impression that he'd worn the socks in order to provoke precisely the reaction she had just provided. She looked across to where Patrick Mulligan sat. The retired policeman glowered at Simon, his craggy features set in their customarily disgruntled expression. He reached for his wallet. Clearly there had been a bet. It was the socks. Agatha rolled her eyes and pushed open the door to her office.

No sooner had she circumnavigated the enormous desk that dominated the small space and dropped her handbag into one of its cavernous drawers than Helen Freedman appeared with a cup of coffee, a document folder and a copy of the *Mircester Telegraph*. Helen was probably the most organised person Agatha had ever met. Middle-aged and thoroughly efficient, she served as Agatha's secretary but also handled most of the day-to-day admin chores.

"Some invoices for your approval," Helen set the coffee, newspaper and folder down on the desk, "a couple of bills to sign off and some rather interesting expenses from Simon."

Noting Helen's raised eyebrows, Agatha thanked her for the coffee and asked her to let the others know there would be a case catch-up meeting in her office in ten minutes. She then sat down to enjoy her coffee and read the story behind the headline "Man Found Dead on Bowling Green."

When the others assembled in her office, dragging in chairs, clutching sheaves of papers and balancing mugs of coffee, the chat was all about the dead man in the park. Agatha dismissed their questions by telling them it looked like some kind of tragic accident, which was greeted with moans of disappointment.

"Agatha Raisin comes across a body and there's not even a hint of foul play?" Simon clutched a hand to his chest in mock incredulity. "Surely that can't be?"

"Well, I found it all more than a bit suspicious," Agatha admitted, "and I am certainly intrigued, but we should wait to hear what the coroner has to say at the inquest on Friday. Now—down to business." She flicked through a file and pulled out a sheet of paper, scanning the page as she spoke. "So, Simon, how are you progressing with the Popplewell case? Background and update, please."

"Well, I've run into a little problem there actually." Simon shifted uncomfortably in his seat. "You might remember that Victor Popplewell has a warehouse—a series of warehouses, actually—from where he runs a distribution business, sending everything from dog food to digital radios all over the country. He sees himself as a good employer, paying his warehouse staff decent wages and generous sick pay."

"I remember meeting him." Agatha nodded. "He treats his staff well so that they will be loyal and there will be no pilfering from shipments."

"Correct." Simon made a clicking noise in his cheek and a little clapping, finger-snapping move that ended with him pointing at her like a game show host awarding the star prize. She hated it when he did that. "One of his warehouse managers, Deirdre Higginbotham, has been taking a lot of time off with a bad back, and even though she has a doctor's note confirming a long-standing problem, he thinks she's taking the pi—"

Agatha scowled at him.

"—taking advantage of his good nature. He asked us to check up on her and I've been keeping her under surveillance."

"So why does this expenses sheet," Agatha held up the paper she had been studying, "have claims on it for entry fees and drinks at the Mata Hari Lounge, Shirley's Girlies and Honeybuns?"

"The strip clubs?" Toni laughed. "You've been visiting strip clubs on expenses?"

Agatha gave her a look of mild surprise.

"What?" Toni shrugged, still smiling. "I know what those clubs are; who doesn't? It's not like I work there."

"No," Simon punctuated his statement with a raised hand, "but I think my subject does. I think Deirdre Higginbotham with the bad back appears on stage as Cindy Snakehips—and there's nothing wrong with Cindy's back, believe me."

"So you think she's taking time off to moonlight as a stripper?" Agatha mused. "That's bad. Not that there's anything wrong with being an exotic dancer—we all have to earn a living—but she shouldn't be doing it while she's claiming sick pay. What proof do you have?"

"None," Simon admitted. "She wears a hood on the way to the clubs and goes in through the staff entrance. I can't follow her in there because there are some very big blokes around to stop you doing that. They're also very unhappy about you taking any photographs. Pay to get in, and there are some even bigger blokes inside who are even less keen on photos."

"But you've seen her dance," said Agatha. "Several times, judging by these drinks bills."

"There's a minimum three-drink charge in those places," Patrick volunteered, then, seeing Agatha's quizzical look, added, "I was a cop. We used to meet informants in places like that."

"Seems like I'm the only one who doesn't know about these clubs." Agatha turned to Simon again. "You saw her on stage, so you can identify her?"

"Not really. She always wore a snakeskin-pattern mask over most of her face."

"She never took it off?"

"It was the only thing she never took off."

"Any distinguishing features?"

"Yes, the tattoo." Simon grinned. "She isn't called Cindy Snakehips only because of how she dances." He swayed from side to side in his seat in a disturbingly snake-like manner. "She has a rattlesnake tattoo with the head on one hip and the tail on the other. The body kind of disappears at the back and then—"

"Thank you, Simon," Agatha cut him short, "but that's probably not a huge help. We can hardly tell Mr. Popplewell to ask Deirdre Higginbotham to show him her rattler next time he sees her. I need to have a think about how we take this forward."

The discussion moved on through a short but busy agenda of cases ranging from the inevitable divorce investigations to disputes between neighbours and the company's regular, bread-and-butter work for insurance companies and other corporate clients.

"All very busy as usual," Agatha commented. "Anything new come in?"

"I took a phone call from a Miss Featherstone, who claims that a man is spying on her in her sitting room," said Toni.

"A peeping Tom?" Agatha asked,

"Not exactly," Toni explained. "She says he comes into the room and watches her."

"Sounds creepy," said Agatha, "but whether he's a peeping Tom or breaking and entering, it's a job for the police, not us."

"She has reported him to the police," Toni glanced down at her notes, "and they came round to investigate but could find no sign of a break-in and no sign of anyone other than her having been in her flat. I checked with them and they said that because no crime had been committed, there was nothing they could do."

"I take it Miss Featherstone is local?" Agatha asked. Toni nodded. "Let's pay her a visit later today. Anything else?"

"A contractor who works for the local council has been in touch," said Patrick in his usual matter-of-fact tone. "They're employed to carry out domestic refuse collection—they operate the bin lorries that collect from households around Mircester. One of the company directors is an old friend and he wants us to look into rumours that his employees are dealing drugs. If it's true, he'll call in the police, of course, but he wants to substantiate the rumours first in order to avoid any unnecessary embarrassment for the company or the council."

"You mean the council would sack them if it turns out that the bin men are dealers?" Simon asked.

"Exactly," Patrick confirmed. "They want someone to go out on the trucks discreetly to find out what's going on."

"Well, Simon," Agatha smiled across the desk at the look of dread spreading across the young man's face, "this is your chance to practise being discreet. Lose the orange socks and sign up as a bin man."

"Riding around in a bin lorry?" Simon groaned. "Really?"

"You're the only one of us who would be believable as an undercover bin man," she pointed out. "Patrick's a bit long in the tooth for that sort of work, and neither Toni nor I really fit the bill. Liaise with Patrick over the details. Are we finished? Good—I need to shift some of this paperwork."

Simon and Patrick filed out of the office, Toni following. She allowed them both to leave before turning back to Agatha.

"There was one more business call," she said. "Sir Charles Fraith."

"What did he want?" Agatha looked up at her suspiciously. "Why didn't he call me on my mobile?"

"He was afraid that you might just hang up on him."

"He was right to be afraid."

"He said that he had a couple of important things to discuss with you. One of them involves a friend of his and a disputed paternity claim."

"I'll see to it, Toni."

"Are you sure? I can deal with him if you like."

"I can handle him, thank you." Agatha's jaw set firm. Could she handle him? The dapper Sir Charles, a former friend and former lover, had played fast and loose with Agatha's feelings and loyalty once too often when the two clashed during a chance meeting at a vineyard in the Gironde. She had promised herself never to let him back in her life again, and she would not. If he needed the professional services of Raisin Investigations, well, that was different. He would receive the same courteous, efficient service as any other client. Yes, she could handle Sir Charles Fraith.

"I don't mean to intrude," Toni went on, "and whatever happened in France is none of my business, but—"

"You're right—it's none of your business."

"I'm sorry, but I don't want you to get hurt again," said Toni. "I'm just concerned that—"

"Don't be!" Agatha snapped. "I'm perfectly capable of looking after myself, thank you very much."

"Okay, have it your way." Toni left the office quickly. She had endured too many powder-keg conversations that inevitably ignited both their tempers to push Agatha any further.

Agatha sighed and turned to the papers on her desk. She knew she had been short with Toni and promised herself she would make it right. Toni was more than just an employee, after all, and it made no sense to fall out with her.

Nothing concerning Charles, however, made any sort of sense any more. That relationship was an emotional minefield. She pushed it all out of her mind by picking up the top envelope from the pile. It was marked PERSONAL.

Opening the envelope, she found a single sheet of paper with a short, typewritten message. She quickly turned the paper over, running her fingertips across the back. It really was typewritten, not a computer-generated, laser-printed pastiche of a typewritten note, the typewriter keys having left indentations on the back of the paper. The message itself was even more intriguing:

```
NOT SUICIDE. NOT AN ACCIDENT.
THE ADMIRAL WAS MURDERED!
```

Just after midday, Agatha tapped on the glass between her office and the main room, catching Toni's attention and signalling her to come in. Looking slightly glum, Toni picked up a notepad and dutifully appeared in front of Agatha's desk.

"Can Miss Featherstone see us today?" Agatha asked.

"Yes, I spoke to her earlier. She's happy for us to visit any time. She'll be in all day."

"Good. We can leave as soon as you're ready." Agatha paused, then added, "Toni, about earlier, I—"

"Oh, you're not going to get all mushy, are you?"

"Mushy?" Agatha tensed and recoiled with a frown. "I do *not* get 'mushy,' whatever that might mean!"

"Good." Toni smiled. "I couldn't stand a mushy Agatha Raisin."

"That's just as well." Agatha relaxed her shoulders. Normally someone daring to tease her would make her tense and defensive. She hated being teased. Someone making fun of you generally meant that someone had got the better of you—that they had won and you had lost, and she *really* hated losing. Toni, however, was different. Her gentle teasing was a way of letting Agatha off the hook—no apology required, no awkwardness necessary. "Now, what do you make of this?"

Agatha handed Toni the envelope marked PERSONAL. Toni turned it over in her hands, examining front and back.

"It's correctly addressed," she noted. "Very neatly done. Looks like it was typed on an old-fashioned typewriter. No stamp or postmark, so it was hand-delivered." She took the sheet of paper out of the envelope and gasped as she unfolded it. "Wow! Someone clearly wants you to take an interest in the bowling green murder."

"Clearly," Agatha agreed, "and that someone would like to remain anonymous."

"What are you going to do?"

"Exactly what I've intended to do ever since I came across the Admiral's body—track down a murderer! Let's deal with Miss Featherstone, then we can head back to the scene of the crime."

Agatha and Toni left the office together to walk to Miss Featherstone's apartment block down by the river on the other side of Mircester city centre. It was not quite lunchtime, but there was a throng of shoppers milling around the high street, enjoying the warm weather and the chance to snap up a few bargains in what all the larger stores were advertising as their "Grand Summer Sale." This latest sale had, in Agatha's opinion, followed with indecent haste after the "Spring Clearance Sale," the "Mad March Sale," the traditional month-long "January Sale," the "Christmas Special Sale" and a host of other sales that stretched back as far as she could remember. The business to be in, she reasoned, the one obviously making the most profit, was the printer who produced all the sale signs and pamphlets.

Leaving the bustle of the shopping centre behind, they took a riverside walk where a grassy bank dropped steeply towards the water on one side, while on the other, municipal flower beds erupting with the joyful colours of marigolds, begonias and petunias basked in the sunshine. They passed a couple of comatose down-and-outs quietly fermenting on a bench, an empty bottle of sherry abandoned on the ground in front of them.

"Sad, isn't it," said Toni, "that drink has destroyed them."

"Drink hasn't destroyed them, Toni." Agatha shook her head. "They destroyed themselves. Drink was their weapon of choice. Whatever problems they may have tried to eradicate with it are probably of little consequence now that their weapon has backfired. The drink is now in control."

"I guess we both know how that works." Toni nodded. There was a short silence. When Toni had first come to work for her, Agatha had helped her to escape from an abusive alcoholic mother. Her own parents had also been hopeless drunks, and her first husband, Jimmy Raisin, had been a thoroughly unpleasant, violent alcoholic.

"Do you think the Admiral was an alcoholic?" Toni asked. "He clearly thought he was drinking rum from that bottle, and it must have been fairly early in the day."

"We'll find out." Agatha nodded. "We need to build up a complete picture of the man in order to find out who would have wanted him dead."

She glanced at the sherry bottle, saw that it was the same brand that she and Margaret Bloxby enjoyed from time to time at the vicarage, and resolved to buy her friend a case of something more upmarket.

Rounding a bend in the path, they came upon the apartment building. A wrought-iron sign standing by the path boldly declared it to be Molyneux Mansions. It was a modern, but attractive, three-storey brick-built complex with balconies looking out over the river, patios serving the ground-floor accommodation and a courtyard scattered with raised flower beds bursting with the same energetic profusion of summer colour they had seen near the riverside walk.

Miss Featherstone's flat was on the second floor, and the stairwell leading up to it was tidy and clean. There was a welcome mat outside her front door and the doorbell played a cheerful chime.

"This is a really nice block of flats," said Toni. "Much better than where I live."

"It's not bad at all, is it?" Agatha agreed, although it was far from the thatch-and-wisteria Cotswolds idyll that had first tempted her away from London to Carsely.

The door was opened by a dark-haired, bespectacled lady whom Agatha judged to be in her late sixties. She was wearing a green cardigan, a fake pearl necklace and a neat tartan skirt.

"You must be Mrs. Raisin," she said, smiling at Agatha, "and you're the young lady I talked to on the phone, Toni, isn't it? Do come in."

She led them along a narrow hallway with doors to the left that led to a bedroom, a bathroom and a kitchen before the passage opened out into a comfortable sitting room. Windows looked out over the river and there was a small balcony. Two armchairs and a sofa that appeared never to have had anything heavier than a dusting cloth weighed upon their floral-pattern cushions were arranged around an electric fire. The decorative wooden fire surround was populated by a variety of ornaments and figurines ranging from a shimmering ballerina to a sorrowful street urchin and a playful kitten. The room was as neat and clean as Miss Featherstone herself. Agatha noted that there were two pull-cords in opposite corners of the room, just as there had been at either end of the hall.

"Do sit down," Miss Featherstone insisted. "I'll fetch some tea. The kettle's just boiled."

Agatha felt almost guilty about denting the sofa cushions, and Toni lowered herself gingerly down beside her.

"The place is spotless," said Toni.

"Immaculate," Agatha agreed. "She seems to take care of herself and her flat very well."

Miss Featherstone swiftly returned with a tea tray that she set down on a small coffee table in front of Agatha and Toni before filling china cups for them both and offering chocolate shortbread biscuits.

"Your flat is gorgeous, Miss Featherstone," said Toni. "How long have you lived here?"

"Since I retired. I had a small house, but the garden was really too much for me to keep tidy."

"You have pull-cords," Agatha said. "Are those to summon help if you need it?"

"That's right," Miss Featherstone explained. "In emergencies, they alert the warden who supervises the apartment block."

"Did you pull one of the cords when the man was in your flat—your intruder?"

"Oh no." Miss Featherstone sounded quite shocked. "The cords are for medical emergencies. I telephoned the police about the man."

"But the police could find no trace of him having been here?" asked Toni.

"Apparently not," Miss Featherstone shrugged, "yet he's been in this room several times."

"How does he get in?" Agatha asked. "Through the balcony door or through the main door?"

"I've never actually seen him use either door," Miss Featherstone admitted. "In the evenings I like to sit and read or watch a little television, and suddenly I'll get that feeling—you know, as if someone's watching you. I'll turn around and he'll be there, standing by the bookcase, or sometimes by the hall door."

"Does he say anything, or do anything?" Toni asked.

"No, he just stands there, staring, hardly moving at all."

"That sounds absolutely terrifying," said Agatha. "Do you scream at him, tell him to get out, or yell for help?"

"I'm usually so frightened," Miss Featherstone's eyes widened alarmingly, "that I can scarcely move, and I daren't scream. I don't know what he might do if I did."

"What does he look like?" asked Toni, making notes on a pad.

"He's always in the shadows," Miss Featherstone waved a hand towards the places where the man usually stood, "and wearing dark clothes. I suppose he looks quite ordinary."

"This is appalling," said Agatha. "We can't allow it to go on. We need to find this man. What if we were to put some little cameras in the corners of the room so that we can get pictures of him?"

"Oh, I don't think that would work." Miss Featherstone shook her head. "He won't show up on cameras. He protects himself from that sort of thing, and from radar. He's from Venus, you see. He parks his spaceship in orbit above Earth and transports himself down here by laser beam. That's why the police said they couldn't catch him."

Toni stopped writing. Agatha froze for an instant, then placed her teacup gently back in its saucer on the coffee table.

38

"Well, Miss Featherstone," she said. "I think we have enough to be going on with, don't we, Toni?"

"Yes, of course," Toni agreed. "We'd best be on our way. I'll be in touch soon, Miss Featherstone."

They said nothing until they were back on the path outside Molyneux Mansions.

"Who did you talk to at Mircester Police about Miss Featherstone, Toni?" Agatha was staring out over the river, her head high and her hands clasped tightly behind her back.

"It was someone new," said Toni, consulting her notepad. "A PC Easeman."

"First name?"

"I believe he said it was Paul." Toni's hands dropped to her sides and she stared at the ground, shaking her head in disbelief. "I can't believe I was had like that."

"You let someone claiming to be a policeman called Paul Easeman send us on a wild goose chase?"

"I'm sorry, Agatha, I should have realised . . ."

Turning to look at her assistant, Agatha unclasped her hands, let out a long breath and growled, "He must have thought he was being *so* clever, having *such* a big laugh at our expense. Well, he'll regret it when I find out exactly who our policeman Paul Easeman really is!"

Toni's face was set in a look of utter dejection. Clearly she felt she had let Agatha down by falling for Paul Easeman's little jape. Paul Easeman—really? Agatha burst out laughing.

"Whoever he is, he's going to need his sense of humour when we work out how to get our own back on him." She smiled, and Toni's face brightened. "Now, let's go find the warden who's in charge here and make sure that they know about poor Miss Featherstone's imaginary visitor from outer space. Then we can walk over to the bowling club to have a sniff around."

Mircester Crown Green Bowling Club was far quieter than it had been when Agatha had last visited. Gone were the inquisitive onlookers, the police officers and the paramedics. Three of the club members were pottering in the rose garden, dead-heading blooms and pulling out weeds. Agatha immediately recognised one of them.

"Good afternoon, Mr. Partridge," she called, waving. "May we come in?"

"Of course, Mrs. Raisin," replied the man with the oyster eyes, flattening his comb-over. "How nice to see you again. You're most welcome."

Agatha introduced Toni, and Stanley Partridge showed them to a bench nestled between a large pink rose bush festooned with flowers and an equally abundant white rose.

"What brings you back here, Mrs. Raisin?" he asked.

"I really liked the look of your lovely club," said Agatha. "It started me thinking that I might take up bowling to keep me occupied when I retire."

"It's a grand sport." Mr. Partridge nodded. "Right sociable it is."

"My goodness." Agatha sniffed the air. "Your roses have a wonderful scent."

"Fragrance is stronger later in the day." Mr. Partridge

nodded and smiled. "The pink is Gertrude Jekyll an' the white is Desdemona. Both are good varieties for fragrance. Desdemona has a more lemony scent—the Jekyll is far sweeter. It's a nice balance in this spot."

"They're beautiful. You certainly know your roses, Mr. Partridge," Agatha congratulated him.

"They give a great deal of pleasure in return for a little effort," he replied.

"It seems very quiet here today," Toni commented.

"The rose garden's always a champion place for a bit of calm," Mr. Partridge chuckled, "even when they're hard at it out on the green."

"Is no one playing today?" Agatha asked.

"No, no, Mrs. Raisin. The police were happy for us to do whatever we liked once they left, but we decided it were right to stop all play for a week. Sort of a mark of respect for the Admiral, you know."

"Did the Admiral enjoy working in the rose garden with you?" Toni sniffed one of the white Desdemonas, then immediately sneezed and scrabbled in her handbag for a tissue.

"He hated the roses." Mr. Partridge shook his head, the corners of his mouth turned down in an expression of disgust. "You might say he were a fine lad in some ways, but he had some right barmy ideas. Can you believe he wanted to rip out all these wonderful bushes and plant vegetables?"

"Why on earth would he want to do that?" Agatha was genuinely appalled.

"Because he had some stupid plan about making rum out of sugar beets and carrots!" Mr. Partridge was becoming

41

agitated. "He'd have done it, too. He were always one to get his own way in the end."

"Did he have much to do with the garden?" Toni dropped her tissue into a litter bin.

"He always acted like he were in charge of everything." Mr. Partridge sounded quietly bitter. "Liked throwing his weight around, he did, telling everyone what's what. The paths were his thing. He kept them neat. Said they was our 'defensive line' to keep weeds from spreading onto the green. He used weedkiller on the paths fairly regular."

"Where did he keep his weedkiller?" Agatha asked.

"In the shed back there." Mr. Partridge pointed over his shoulder. "The police took a quick look. I'll show you."

He led them down a paved walkway through the rose bushes to the tool shed Agatha had seen on her previous visit. Inside, the sun fought its way through murky windows, shafts of light picking out the tiniest motes of dust drifting in the air and wafting through the open door. Mr. Partridge pointed to a collection of Smuggler's Breath rum bottles standing in a neat row on a shelf at the very back of the shed. There were six full bottles and one half full.

"That's where he kept the stuff." The old man's face looked grim again. "It weren't a normal brand. Powerful stuff. Very poisonous. Been banned in this country for years, but he bought it off some dodgy bloke at Mircester Market. He claimed he kept it in them bottles as a measure—one bottle would treat all the paths."

"You don't sound like you believe that's why he used the rum bottles," Toni noted.

"It may well have been one reason," Mr. Partridge nodded, "but he also used them bottles so as no one knew what it were. He didn't want to get caught with the illegal weedkiller. We all knew it weren't rum in the bottles, of course. I mean—who keeps a shelf of rum bottles in a garden shed? Mind you, one or two actually did have rum in them. He were a devil for his rum. I warned him that having weedkiller in them bottles were a bad idea. Too easy to get his rum mixed up with his weedkiller. In the end, it looks like that's what happened. It were a nasty accident."

"If this stuff is illegal," Agatha pondered, "why didn't the police take it all away?"

"They didn't spend too much time at the club," Mr. Partridge explained. "That young sergeant . . . um . . ."

"Sergeant Wong?" Agatha suggested.

"That's the fellow," Mr. Partridge agreed. "He had his boys and girls on their hands and knees going over the whole bowling green and garden. He were doing a proper job. Then the older policeman showed up again."

"DCI Wilkes?" asked Toni.

"Yes, him," said Mr. Partridge. "He ordered them all out because he needed them somewhere else. He never gave them a chance to search back here."

"Do you think it really was an accident?" Agatha examined the bottles, unscrewing the cap on the one that was half full and taking a sniff. It was definitely weedkiller, not rum. "Did the Admiral have any enemies—anyone who hated him enough to want him dead?"

"I'm sorry, Mrs. Raisin," said Mr. Partridge, suddenly

seeming more than a little flustered, "but I need to get back to the roses. I have to finish that bed this afternoon, you see, and . . ."

"We'll let you get on with it, then." Agatha smiled. "Thank you, Mr. Partridge."

They followed the old man back through the rose garden and waved farewell from the gate.

"He seemed like a nice man," said Toni as they walked back towards their office, "but he got really nervous when you asked him whether anyone hated the Admiral."

"I think the direct question caught him off guard," Agatha agreed. "Clearly there are people around here who were not fans of the Admiral, including Mr. Partridge himself."

"And what was all that about you retiring?"

"Forget it, Toni." Agatha made a chopping gesture with her hand as though to cut off the thought. "That's never going to happen."

Chapter Three

James Lacey paused on the pavement outside the antiques shop that sat below Raisin Investigations' first-floor office. A red military drum draped with white rope sitting alongside a British infantry "stovepipe" shako hat had caught his eye. A former army officer, James frowned at the regimental badges on each, taking no more than a second to dismiss them as fakes. Then he saw his own reflection, not in the shop window but in a large, elaborately gilded mirror standing behind the drum. He drew himself up to his full height and smoothed a palm over the front of his sports jacket. He considered himself still to have a military bearing. He was tall, well over six feet, but carried his slim frame upright, shoulders set square with no hint of a stoop. His dark hair had picked up a trace of grey in recent years, but unlike so many of his old army chums, he still had plenty of it. In his estimation, he was shaping up pretty well. Agatha was a fine-looking woman, but surely he was a worthy partner for her? He still had a youthful twinkle in his blue eyes, didn't he? He moved his head left and right, searching for a twinkle, squeezing his eyes closed and then popping them open

45

in an effort to generate one. That was when he saw Mr. Tinkler watching him with a very peculiar look on his face. He smiled sheepishly, gave him a curt nod and moved on.

The rest of her team having left for the day, Agatha was alone in the office when the entryphone buzzer sounded. During the day, the street door was generally left unlocked, but she knew that one of the others would have slipped the latch as they left, to keep her secure on her own outside normal office hours. It was a kind thought, but it meant that she would have to leave the case files spread out on her desk and cross to the outer office to answer the buzzer. She decided to ignore it. She was trying to concentrate. It buzzed again. She tutted, jumped to her feet and thundered across the floor to jab her thumb on the answer button.

"We're closed!" she snapped. "Go away!"

"That's not very good customer relations," came James's voice.

"And you're not a customer, James. What do you want?"

"Can I come up?"

"No."

Agatha released the button and the buzzer immediately sounded again. She sighed, knowing that he wasn't going to give up, and pressed the button to unlock the door. His footsteps echoed up the stairwell, taking each tread with military precision, marching double time.

"Good evening," he said, smiling as he entered the office. "What are you doing working so late?"

"It's hardly late, James. It's barely seven o'clock."

"But you have had a rather long day. You left quite early this morning."

"Am I under observation now? I thought snooping on people was supposed to be my job, not yours." Agatha folded her arms and cocked her head to one side.

"I was having a coffee and looking out over the front garden," James defended himself. "I couldn't help noticing you leave."

"So what brings you here at this time of day? I can't remember the last time you were in my office."

"Oh, I can!" he offered brightly. "We were still married at the time and—"

"Yes, all right, James. I don't actually need to know when you were last here. I'd like to know what you're doing here now. I have reports to finish going through."

"Well, it's a surprise!" With the hesitant flourish of a second-rate stage magician, James whisked a leaflet from an inside jacket pocket. "There's a new bistro opened in Evesham run by a chap called Marco, and since I am an esteemed travel writer and restaurant aficionado, he has offered me a very special rate for dinner for two!"

Agatha paused for a moment to consider the invitation. She hardly felt flattered to be considered as a cut-price date, but she had stuck rigidly to her calorie-controlled lunch, and her stomach had been making alarming rumbling noises for the past half-hour.

"So how about it?" James waggled the leaflet. "I'm told this place is outstanding. I'll admit, it was Marco himself who told me that, but he seems like a thoroughly decent chap and I believe him to be entirely trustworthy."

"Oh James." Agatha smiled, unsure whether she was giving in to his persistence or her own hunger pangs. "I'm sure it will be lovely. Give me a moment to finish up here."

James triumphantly tucked the leaflet back in his pocket and took a seat at Helen Freedman's desk, just outside Agatha's office. The phone rang and, buoyed by high-spirited enthusiasm, he reached for the receiver, despite Agatha gesticulating frantically from behind her desk for him to leave it alone.

"Raisin Investigations," he said in a sober voice that belied the smile on his face. "How may we help you? You have what? Really? Please hold the line, sir, Mrs. Raisin is right here. I will put you on loudspeaker."

Agatha stomped out of her office, scowling at James.

"Please can you repeat that for Mrs. Raisin's benefit, sir?"

"Yes, of course." The man's voice was a flat nasal drone, delivering his answer in an almost emotionless tone. "I'd like your help to find out why strange creatures keep appearing in my garden. Last week I saw three small wizards dressed all in black, with orange hats and long white beards. Then I saw the spirit of Aslan."

"Aslan?" James was struggling to keep a straight face. Agatha rolled her eyes and turned to go back into her office. "The lion from *The Lion, the Witch and the Wardrobe*?"

"The very same. Large as life, he was, and pale white like a ghost. Now I've got the giant grinning rats."

Agatha stopped, turned back and mouthed, "He's got what?" in disbelief.

"I'm sorry, sir, would you mind repeating that?" James's voice was politely serious, but his expression was full of laughter.

"Giant grinning rats," said the caller. "There was a bunch of them on my lawn yesterday evening. I was trying to watch telly, but they kept peering in through the patio door—and grinning at me."

"Have you tried calling the police about these creatures, sir?" James asked.

"Of course I have. After Aslan, they said they thought I was crackers."

"I agree with them," Agatha muttered.

"So what happened with the grinning rats, sir?" James enquired, clearly enjoying himself.

"Well, I went out to chase them away," the man explained, "and they all legged it. I got close to one of them, and it pulled a baby out of its pocket, dropped it on the lawn and scarpered."

"Oh, did it?" To Agatha's surprise, James's face now reflected the concern in his voice and he sat upright, suddenly alert. "What happened to the baby?"

"I've still got it," said the man. "Haven't a clue what to do with the little blighter."

"Can you give me your name and address?" James asked, scribbling furiously on a notepad. "That's great, Mr. Collins. We'll be with you in about half an hour. If the grinning rats show up again, don't chase them away. Promise? Good. See you shortly."

"What are you playing at, James?" Agatha growled through pursed lips. "First you offer to take me out for a distinctly unflattering bargain-basement dinner, and now you've committed us to visiting someone who clearly needs to see a shrink rather than a private detective. I've already wasted time on one complete fiasco today. I've no intention of chasing any more wild geese!"

"Bear with me, Aggie." James held up a calming hand. "This chap's house is on the road to Evesham, so it won't really take us out of our way, and if I'm right, it could be very interesting."

They took Agatha's car, James having caught a bus from Carsely to Mircester in the hope that they would be driving back to Lilac Lane together. He'd had second thoughts about the bus when it took him all round the council housing estate just outside Carsely picking up an assortment of hoodie-clad youths wearing jeans and tracksuit trousers that appeared to be falling down. They collapsed across numerous seats, grunting and shouting at each other while their thumbs flicked like pinball flippers across their phone screens. James sat straight and tall in his seat, uncomfortably conscious that his shirt and tie were attracting stares of derision yet pleased that, unlike the posse of youngsters, his underwear was not on display.

James drove, Agatha making it crystal clear that, having

already endured an encounter that day with someone who believed she was being visited by a peeping Tom from Venus, there was no way she was spending time with another wacko, followed by a discount dinner, without the compensation of being able to look forward to a couple of glasses of wine. James was happy to forgo a drink, and his voluntary abstinence brought their conversation round to the Admiral's drinking habits and the bowling green murder.

"Apart from the note," said James, "what evidence do you have that the Admiral was murdered?"

"None, really," Agatha admitted, "and it's possible—not very likely, but possible—that he could have been so drunk that he didn't realise he was swigging weedkiller."

"But you don't believe that? You don't believe it was an accident?"

"It just never felt like an accident, and the more I hear about this man, the more I'm convinced that there are people who might want him dead. He certainly seemed to divide opinion at the bowling club. One woman there described him as 'an absolute monster.'"

"Then you should follow your instincts and treat it as a murder."

"You seem very keen for me to get involved."

"Of course I am. You are far more interesting to be around when you're on the trail of a murderer."

Agatha gave James a quizzical look.

"So I'm a bit boring the rest of the time, am I?" There was no disguising the vexatious edge to her voice.

"Never in a million years!" James smiled. "Agatha Raisin

is never, *ever* boring, but with a murder on your hands, the real Agatha comes to the fore."

"I suppose you're right," she said. She *knew* he was right. She had been feeling that frisson of excitement ever since she opened the anonymous note. If she was honest with herself, she'd been feeling it from the moment she saw the Admiral lying on the bowling green. Perhaps she felt a little guilty about that. Should she really relish the thought that someone had been murdered? That hardly seemed right. Yet catching a murderer was certainly the right thing to do, and she was really rather good at that. She quelled her excitement with thoughts of Mr. Collins's giant grinning rats, and gazed out of the window at the passing countryside.

Leaving Mircester, they joined the A44 towards Evesham. In the soft evening light, the hedgerows, in full leaf at this time of year, almost turned the road into a shady green tunnel. Where the roadside vegetation fell away, there were expansive views across the Vale of Evesham's fertile fields all the way to the Malvern Hills in the far distance. They passed a signpost for the Broadway Tower. Agatha smiled. She had visited the tower only once; it was a splendid folly—a miniature castle sixty-five feet high, standing on one of the highest points in the area. It had been built by the Earl of Coventry more than two hundred years ago in order to please his second wife, Barbara, so the story went. Barbara had wondered if it would be possible to see a signal fire on the hill from their mansion near Pershore some twenty miles away. In the end, she could.

Agatha imagined the relief the earl must have felt when

they viewed the flickering light of the signal. Barbara didn't sound like the kind of woman you'd want to disappoint. Neither, however, was Agatha Raisin. She glanced across at James, who was guiding the car onto a narrow side road. In many ways, she had been far more enamoured of him when he had first moved into the cottage next door to hers. Then, he was a tall, handsome stranger and she had pursued him with unrelenting determination. The fact that he had been slightly aloof and reluctant to become involved only spurred her on.

She remembered the elation she had felt when he had agreed to pose as her husband to help investigate the murder of a young hiker. She remembered too the thrill of excitement that had fired her infatuation. Sadly, their actual marriage had been a disaster. Maybe they had both been too set in their ways to share their lives so completely. At the time, neither of them had any real regrets about divorcing. Yet as time passed, they had remained close, as friends and neighbours. Clearly there was still a bond between them, and when Agatha had suggested that their divorce might have been a mistake, James had readily agreed. He had shown her nothing but kindness, becoming an ever more important part of her life ever since. Was she really ready to commit to him again? More importantly at this particular point in time, with the car slowing gently to a halt, was she really ready for Mr. Collins and his imaginary menagerie?

"This is it," said James, switching off the engine. "Seems like a well-kept house."

"That," said Agatha, recalling her experience earlier in

the day, "means precisely nothing." She had to admit, however, that the house had a great deal of charm. The last rays of the sun played on stone walls that supported a perfectly tiled roof. Two windows on the ground floor and three on the upper floor boasted immaculate white wooden frames with no sign of cracked or peeling paint. The open porch sheltering the gleaming red front door was almost engulfed with the delightful yellow blooms of a climbing rose.

A portly man who appeared to be in his seventies opened the door. He was wearing a comfortably old grey cardigan and grey trousers, and was just tall enough for the top of his head to reach James's shoulder. They made their introductions and he led them inside.

"You have a lovely home, Mr. Collins," James complimented the old man as they walked into the lounge. The room ran from the front to the rear of the house, where floor-to-ceiling glass doors opened onto a patio.

Agatha scanned her surroundings. There was a large dark brown sofa and two oversized armchairs, each of which was embellished with a selection of floral scatter cushions. A gilded mirror sat on a mantelpiece above a well-used open fireplace. The mantelpiece was adorned with an array of family photographs featuring children in the various uniforms of their young lives, from christening robes and school blazers to university graduation gowns and wedding outfits. Similar photographs decorated the walls and stood proudly on small side tables and a long dresser. The room was not to Agatha's taste, but it was clean, tidy and not at all what she had been expecting. It was a normal, comfortable room, not the shambolic surroundings of a fantasist who was losing his marbles. On the other hand—she felt herself shrug—Miss Featherstone's apartment had also been a neat, tidy place. You couldn't always judge a book by its cover, or a person by the place where they lived.

"Thank you, Mr. Lacey." Mr. Collins straightened with pride. "Please call me Eric. I don't stand much on ceremony, but I do like to keep this old house in order. Our children grew up here and it's been a happy place. I suppose I should have given it up for something smaller when my missus passed on, but I couldn't bear to leave. The kids have moved away but they love coming home, and the grandchildren enjoy running around in the garden. I can't let the little 'uns come here with these creatures roaming around, though."

There it was again, Agatha thought to herself. The man's fixation on the imaginary creatures in his garden seemed starkly at odds with his otherwise orderly lifestyle. Intrigued, she decided to cut to the chase.

"Can you show us the baby giant grinning rat, Eric?" she asked.

"Of course," Eric replied. "Come through to the kitchen."

The kitchen was large, with wood-faced storage units around the walls and blue-tiled work surfaces. It was even more neat and clean than the lounge, with the exception of one corner where the blue tiles were covered with a well-worn towel on which sat a wire cage that Agatha judged to be about the size of a case of wine. It was illuminated by a strong reading lamp.

"He's been sleeping a fair bit, but he ought to be awake

by now," said Eric, stooping to peer into the cage. Agatha stooped alongside him. Inside the cage, staring back at her with large dark eyes, was the most delightful little animal she had ever seen. It had a pear-shaped furry brown face, two dainty round ears sitting on top of its head, a black button nose and a mouth that appeared to be . . . smiling.

As a child, Agatha had never had pets, and for most of her adult life she'd had neither the time nor the inclination to share her home with any kind of animal. When she had been given her cats, Boswell and Hodge, she had eventually warmed to them as much for their independent nature as for their companionship, and at one time she had become rather fond of an irascible flatulent donkey. In the main, however, she regarded herself as a people person rather than a pet person. The fluffy baby in the cage, however, was different. Even though she considered herself to be made of sterner stuff, she felt her heart give a little skip and found herself smiling back at him simply because he was *just . . . so . . . cute!*

"The lamp's to help keep him warm," Eric explained. "The old cage was for the kids' hamsters."

"Well I never." James squatted to see directly into the cage. "I didn't think it could be possible, but what you have there, Eric, is a quokka."

"A what?" Agatha turned to him with raised eyebrows.

"A quokka," James repeated. "It's a kind of miniature wallaby—very rare and found only on the western coast of Australia, mainly on small isolated islands. Because they look like they're smiling, they're known as 'the world's happiest animals.'"

"You've seen them on one of your travel writing trips, haven't you?" Agatha guessed.

"Yes, but I would never have expected to see one here. They're a protected species. They're very friendly, but to stop them becoming ill or catching any kind of infection, tourists are banned from feeding or touching them. No one's allowed to take them home as pets. The clue was when Eric told us about this little chap being abandoned by his mother. That's a survival reaction. To escape from a predator, a mother carrying a baby in her pouch will leave the young one behind to avoid them both becoming somebody's supper."

"He seems partial to lettuce himself," Eric commented, and as if on cue, the quokka picked up a scrap of lettuce to nibble. "I also gave him a bit of warm milk from the finger of a rubber washing-up glove. Reckoned if he was in the pocket, he wouldn't be weaned."

"That's good thinking," James agreed, "but he might need more than just ordinary cow's milk. We need expert help with him. Have you contacted any of the local animal rescue centres?"

"Not yet." Eric sighed. "I'm afraid folks will just think I'm batty, like the police did after I reported Aslan and the wizards."

"Don't worry, Eric," Agatha assured him. "They'll believe me. We'll get you some help with your quokka."

"The babies are called joeys," James said.

"Well, we'll get you some help with little Joey."

"Thank you, Mrs. Raisin." Eric reached across and

squeezed Agatha's hand. "For a while, I thought I might be going crazy. I'm not short of a bob or two, you know. I want to pay you to find out what's going on around here."

"Well, your giant grinning rats are real," Agatha pondered, "so we can assume that Aslan and the wizards are real, too. Any ideas on those, James?"

"Let's take a look." James retrieved his smartphone from his jacket pocket and connected to the internet. "A ghostly white lion . . . what might that be, I wonder?" His fingers tapped the screen and he eventually came up with an image. "Did he look like this?"

Agatha and Eric leaned together to look at the picture on the phone's screen. Haunting green eyes stared out at them from a lion's pale face, its noble head surrounded by a mane like a cloud of snow.

"That's him—that's the ghost of Aslan!" Eric declared.

"Is that some kind of albino lion?" asked Agatha.

"No," said James. "It's a Timbavati white lion from South Africa. Very rare, but they have four at the West Midlands Safari Park, not too far from here."

"Eric's Aslan can't be one of theirs," Agatha pointed out. "I went there once for a corporate function and was given a tour. Their security is top-notch. I don't believe anything could escape. In any case, if a lion was on the loose in the Cotswolds, there would be a huge hue and cry."

"You're right," James nodded, "and nothing has been reported in the media."

"Which might mean that it escaped from someone who

didn't want any fuss being made," said Agatha. "Someone who's not supposed to be in possession of such an animal."

"I see what you're getting at." James nodded. "The lion and the quokkas may have escaped from someone illegally buying and selling exotic species."

"What about the small wizards with beards and orange hats?" Eric asked.

"If we're thinking of animals for the illegal pet trade, these might fit the bill." James produced an image on his phone of a creature with a dark coat, a long white beard and a flash of orange fur on its forehead topped by a flat brush of black hair that looked like an elaborate ceremonial hat.

"What on earth is that?" asked Agatha, peering at the screen.

"That's one of my wizards!" Eric was overjoyed.

"It's a De Brazza's monkey," James explained. "They come from central Africa. I was reading about them the other day. Apparently, they are highly prized as pets."

"Why can't people just stick to cats, dogs and canaries?" Agatha sighed.

"Look!" Eric pointed out of the kitchen window to the rear garden. "They're back!"

Hopping out onto the lawn were half a dozen quokkas, nibbling the grass, investigating the plants in the borders and looking up towards the window with smiles on their faces.

"Why have they suddenly appeared now?" Agatha asked.

"My guess would be that they've been sheltering somewhere safe during the day." James moved closer to the window to get a better look. "Dusk is a favourite time for them to go foraging."

"Let's go outside," Agatha suggested. "We might be able to see how they got into the garden."

Eric opened the kitchen door and they made their way slowly and quietly out onto the lawn, taking care not to alarm the quokkas. The little animals watched them approach, allowed them to come within a few yards, then turned tail and hopped up the garden, disappearing into a barrier of azalea and rhododendron bushes.

"What's beyond those bushes?" Agatha asked.

"There's a tumbledown fence," said Eric. "Keep meaning to fix it up, but out of sight is out of mind and all that . . ."

"And on the other side of the fence?" James was looking for a way through the bushes.

"Not much—the edge of a forest leads off towards fields and a farmyard."

"We need to take a look," said Agatha, and stepped towards the bushes, only for James to catch her arm.

"Not in those things you don't," he said, pointing at her black patent-leather high heels.

"You're right—they'll be ruined if it's muddy," she agreed.

"No." James shook his head. "I meant that you're likely to break your ankle trudging through the woods in those."

"Wait just a minute," Eric said, dodging into a garden shed. "Try these." He reappeared holding a pair of bright red wellington boots with large yellow flowers painted on them. He saw Agatha eyeing the boots with a look that was somewhere between contempt and revulsion. "My daughter keeps them here for when she's playing in the garden with her kids," he explained. "The kids all like to paint their wellies . . ."

"They'll be perfect." Agatha sounded more like she was trying to convince herself than thank the old man. She reminded herself that she had to get her priorities straight when embarking on a new case, and now, as so often before, that meant putting the needs of the investigation above her personal dignity. She slipped into the rubber boots and followed James through a gap in the bushes.

Once beyond the old fence and in amongst the trees, the light began to fade. They made their way through the gloom, heading for a more open area that appeared to be some kind of access track. Suddenly James stopped, raised his right hand above his shoulder and dropped to one knee, crouching behind a fallen tree trunk.

"What do you think you're doing?" Agatha stood over him. "This isn't one of your old army exercises, you know."

James reached for her arm and guided her down beside him, fixing her with his eyes and holding a finger to his lips.

"Quiet," he whispered. "Listen."

Agatha squatted gingerly, listening with great care as much for the dreaded rip of a splitting seam as for anything else. Then she heard heavy footsteps tromping through the undergrowth up ahead, and the sound of angry guttural voices. James pointed, and, squinting through the gathering dusk, Agatha could see half a dozen shadowy figures—men, judging by their size and the way they moved—making their way through the trees, some poking at the vegetation with sticks, some bent almost double. As they drew closer, they were loud enough for her to hear plainly, although she couldn't understand what was being said.

"Sounds eastern European," James said softly.

"Romanian, I'd say," Agatha breathed. She'd once spent the first part of a warm summer in London with Romanian builders working on an apartment block just a stone's throw from her office window. The younger ones had looked quite decorative with their shirts off in the sunshine, but none of them had seemed capable of conversing at anything less than foghorn level. Bawling at them, threatening them and even squirting them with a water pistol rarely quietened them for more than a few minutes, so she had walked into her local travel agent's office and told her she wanted to book a holiday, leaving immediately. When asked where she would like to go, she'd said, "Anywhere but Romania," and the travel agent had looked out of her window at the building site, nodding with complete understanding. A trip to a quiet, peaceful Greek island had ensued.

"They're searching for something," said James.

"Our quokkas, no doubt," Agatha agreed.

Then came a command in English, and the figures stopped.

"Get back here, you useless pillocks!" a furious male voice yelled. "We've got four of them. We'll leave traps for the rest tomorrow."

There was the sound of a diesel engine clattering to life, car doors slamming and a vehicle moving off. Agatha leant an arm on the fallen tree to steady herself, craning her neck to see a Land Rover bumping off down the track. Its headlights flicked on, illuminating the route ahead of it, and she watched the red taillights bouncing and swaying down the rough track until they disappeared out of sight round a bend.

"We have to find out where they went," she said.

"Not too far is my guess." James brushed a dry leaf off his jacket. "The quokkas are unlikely to have roamed any great distance . . . Agatha, your arm . . ."

Agatha looked down and saw, to her horror, a riot of many-legged scaly creatures scuttling around on the sleeve of her jacket. She squealed in disgust, holding her arm rigid and pleading with James to deal with them.

"They're only wood lice," he said calmly, sweeping them off with an open hand. "They're harmless. Nothing to worry about. There—they're gone."

Agatha regained her composure, checking her sleeve, then froze, her eyes widening.

"They're not gone, James," she hissed with growing alarm. "You've brushed them into my welly! I can feel them. They're round my ankle! They're between my toes!"

Hopping on one leg, she held the insect-infested boot out towards him.

"Get them out!" she demanded. "Get them out!"

"Hold still," said James, grabbing hold of the heel and toe

63

of the boot. "I'll pull it off and empty them all out." He gave the boot a tug; it shot off Agatha's foot, and she flew backwards to land in a heap on the forest floor.

"I'm so sorry." He rushed to her side, gently helping her to sit up and casually plucking a twig from her hair. "Are you all right, my dear?"

"I'll survive," Agatha grumbled. James helped her to her feet and she ran her hands over her clothes, brushing away moss and leaves. "Are they all gone? There's nothing else crawling on me, is there?"

"You're fine," he assured her, kneeling in front of her while she balanced on one leg, her hands on his shoulders as he fitted the boot back on her foot. "That's better," he said, rising to stand directly in front of her. "Cinderella, you shall go to the ball."

"Oh James," she sighed, plucking various unidentifiable items of woodland detritus from her skirt and jacket. "Do I look absolutely frightful?"

"Not a bit of it," he said gently, brushing flakes of wood bark from her shoulder. "You never look anything less than absolutely beautiful."

Then, perhaps overcome by the way they were standing so close, perhaps overwhelmed by the romance of being alone together in the forest with the sun setting, he took her face in his hands, leaned forward and kissed her.

After a moment, they pulled apart, each a little surprised. Agatha was surprised because such a moment of unbridled affection was not like the old James. He had never been given to impetuous displays of emotion. This was some-

64

thing new. She was also surprised because she had been caught off guard and hadn't seen the kiss coming. Normally she could read the signs, predict what was about to happen and be thoroughly prepared when a man made his move. Being unprepared was not like the old Agatha. Yet most of all she was surprised because . . . she had liked it. She had felt a tingle, a spark of passion that she had never imagined could ever again play a part in the cosy, convenient relationship she shared with James.

James was surprised at himself for having taken such a bold step, then surprised at Agatha as, without uttering a word, she reached up and kissed him again. There was a moment of silence when their lips parted.

"So . . . um . . . where do we go from here?" he said.

"Back to Eric's place," Agatha laughed. "I want my shoes back. Then we'd best head home. My suit must be covered in muddy marks, and the knees of your trousers are damp and green. We look like we've been—"

"Sharing a romantic moment in the woods?"

"That kind of crept up on us, didn't it?"

"A complete ambush, I'd say." He put an arm round her shoulders and they began to make their way back through the trees. "I'll call Marco and tell him we'll visit his bistro another time."

"That would be best. I'm still hungry, though. How about we go home to Carsely, get changed and cleaned up, then head down to the Red Lion for dinner to celebrate?"

"What exactly are we celebrating?"

"A tingle."

"A tingle? I'm not sure I understand. Is that a good thing?"

"Oh, you'd be surprised." She stopped, put her arms around his neck and they kissed again.

"I never used to like surprises," he grinned, "but I think I may be changing my mind."

"So it's dinner at the Red Lion," Agatha said, leading the way back towards the fence, "to celebrate and lay plans for tomorrow. We need to come back and find out what's going on with the Romanians."

"Absolutely," said James. "We have to follow up on what we saw this evening, and the Red Lion sounds just the ticket. No more surprises tonight."

"Well, you never know . . ." Agatha looked back at him and raised an eyebrow.

"Find anything in there?" Eric's voice came from beyond the rhododendrons.

"Yes," James called back. "I think we did."

There would certainly have been one further surprise for James had he looked up, as unknown to either him or the Romanians, quokkas are perfectly capable of climbing trees. One was sitting on a low branch just above their heads, smiling down on them.

Chapter Four

Her sunglasses rested lightly on her face, and from where she lay on the lounger she could see, through half-closed eyes, a seemingly endless expanse of golden yellow sand stretching so far into the distance that it faded into a blue haze, merging softly with the cloudless sky. She felt the sun's rays warming her skin and knew without looking, just by the feel of it, that she was wearing the blue bikini with the silver sparkles. She was glad that she'd managed to slim down enough to fit into it with confidence. It felt good. A gentle breeze drifted lazily up from the water's edge, carrying a scent of lilac—unusual for the seaside—and taunting her occasionally with a whisper of spray from a wave that had collapsed a little too energetically onto the beach. She knew he was down there, cooling off in the sea, and that he'd be back momentarily, telling her how glorious the water was, and how wonderful she looked lying in the sun, and how—

Her musings were dashed by the sound of a phone ringing. Who on earth brought a phone to an idyllic spot like this and let it ring that loud? It sounded just like the phone on her bedside table at home. Hang on . . . it *was* the phone on her bedside table.

Agatha lifted her head from the pillow, filled with drowsy disappointment that the fantasy beach was merely a dream she'd probably never be able to revisit. She reached out and grabbed the phone, opening one eye to check the time on the radio alarm's digital display. It was barely quarter to eight in the morning. Who on earth could be ringing her at this hour? Then she heard Alice Peters's perky voice.

"Good morning, Agatha. I'm so glad I caught you before you left for work. I know you're an early riser."

"Yes, of course." Agatha ran her tongue over her teeth and took a sip of water from the glass by her bed to help get her mouth working. "Never one to laze around in bed all morning."

"You said the other day that you'd be happy to meet up for a drink and a chat," Alice went on, "but I've been working awful shifts. I don't finish until eight in the evening."

"That's not so bad," said Agatha. "Why don't we pop out for a spot of supper after that?"

"I'd like that. Are you free this evening?"

They arranged to meet at a wine bar in Mircester, and Agatha placed the receiver back in its cradle. She looked round, admiring the way the morning sun cast pleasing shadows from the sloping ceiling of her cottage bedroom across the walls and floor. It was a comfortable, comforting room where she felt relaxed and safe. Yet she had had more than just the room to comfort her last night. James had been here with her, but now, as was his habit, he was gone—up at dawn and off back next door to his own house. She glanced down at the pillow where he had slept next to her and saw a sprig of pinkish-purple lilac. Picking it up, she twirled it in her fingers and savoured the fragrance. This was where the scent of lilac on her beach had come from. James Lacey, she thought, you old romantic. Most of the lilac in their little street—Lilac Lane—was now starting to turn brown, but this sprig was perfect. He must have sneaked out to find it *so* early not to have disturbed her, and—she glanced at the radio alarm again—he had turned that thing off to let her sleep in. Was it James frolicking in the sea during her beach dream? She couldn't picture him there and the dream was now fading fast. She hoped it had been him.

Swinging her legs out of bed, she sniffed the air, picking up the smell of fresh coffee. What an angel! He had left her coffee, too! She pulled on a dressing gown and made her way down to the kitchen, spotting her cats, Boswell and Hodge, sunning themselves in the back garden. They hadn't been upstairs making a racket, jumping on the bed and pestering her, which meant that James must already have fed them. She could easily get used to being pampered like this. Now, however, she had to run through her morning routine on fast-forward to make up for lost time. She grabbed a cup of coffee and headed back upstairs.

Half an hour later, having showered and done her hair

and make-up with a breathtaking speed and efficiency that would leave lesser women in awe, she was on her way down her garden path, making for her car. She was dressed in a black sweater, black trousers, and black walking shoes she sometimes used at weekends, and was clutching two black handbags, one substantially bigger than the other, along with a zipped-up dress carrier. Pottering in his front garden, James waved and called a cheery good morning. Had he been expecting gracious thanks for his efforts earlier that morning, he would have been disappointed, but he understood that Agatha Raisin in a hurry would have no time for niceties.

"I'm running behind time!" she yelled. "Meet me at the office at ten o'clock. I want to see where the Romanians are operating from—discreet surveillance. Don't be late!"

He nodded and smiled as she flung her bags into her car. This was Agatha Raisin operating in top gear, a whirlwind of black cashmere and cotton. He knew there would now be a dozen problems dancing around in her mind, and that by the time she reached her office, she would have found solutions to most of them, ready to instruct her team. Until then, she would be all but oblivious to anything else. Then came a complete surprise that stopped him in his tracks. Just before she stepped into her car, Agatha paused, produced the sprig of lilac, threw him a dazzling smile and blew him a kiss.

"Something's put Mrs. Raisin in a good mood this morning." The grinning postman handed James his gas bill as Agatha's car disappeared down Lilac Lane.

"Ah . . ." James realised that his mouth was open. "Something surely has."

Later that morning, having parked at Eric Collins's house and made their way past his rhododendrons, Agatha and James trudged through the forest, retracing their steps from the evening before. Agatha was carrying the larger of her handbags, while James was wearing a waxed jacket with bulging pockets and military-style cargo trousers with equally well-stuffed pockets. Slung over his shoulder was a brown leather binoculars case.

"What have you got in all those pockets?" Agatha asked.

"Maps, compass, GPS, torch, that sort of thing."

"A torch? In broad daylight?"

"You should always be prepared," James said seriously.

"You're such a Boy Scout sometimes." Agatha shook her head, then stopped when she spotted the track where they had seen the Land Rover. "There's the path, but what are those things near the bushes?"

"They look like traps," said James, peering this way and that. "There's no one around. Let's go take a look."

The traps were cages with an open door and various types of juicy leaves left inside as bait.

"The quokka hops in through the door," James said, pointing, "then it slams shut when the animal's weight on the floor springs a trigger."

"At least they're not using some horrible kind of wire noose or steel clamp."

"That wouldn't be in their interest at all. They would end up with damaged goods. I did some ferreting around on the internet. Each of the quokkas could be worth up to five thousand pounds."

"Really?" Agatha was astounded. "What about the little wizards and Aslan?"

"A De Brazza might be as much as ten thousand and a Timbavati lion far more than that. A cub could fetch in excess of a hundred thousand."

"So this is big business." Agatha nodded, then set off along the track. "Come on—the Land Rover went this way."

They made their way down the track until it wound its way out of the forest, the trees parting to reveal a pattern of undulating fields swooping off to the distant horizon. On their left was a vast field of plants cultivated in long rows. The leafy green foliage sat on ridges separated by shallow trenches and boasted pretty white and yellow flowers.

"Potatoes," said James. "They didn't go that way. It would be easy to see if that lot had been disturbed."

"This way, then," said Agatha, opening a gate into a grassy field that fell away towards a cluster of buildings partly hidden by a hedge and a screen of conifers. "Is that some kind of farmyard?"

"Barns and storage, probably," said James. "Hard to tell. I can't see an actual farmhouse."

"We can follow the hedge." Agatha pointed out their route. "If we keep our heads down, we won't be seen from any of the buildings."

They trotted along the hedge until they came to a gap

through which the Land Rover must have passed. Beyond it, in front of the conifers, was a tall chain-link fence. They dashed to the fence and crouched under cover behind a grassy mound.

"That's how the Land Rover got through." James pointed to a gate held fast by a chain and padlock.

"And this will be how the animals got out." Agatha tugged at a weave of barbed wire that had been used to close some damaged sections of the fence. "This fence is pretty old. Looks like they've patched up a few holes. We need to get through to those trees to see down towards the buildings."

"We're bound to be spotted if we try climbing over," James pointed out, looking up at the unwelcoming jagged edge at the top of the high fence.

"Be prepared, Boy Scout," Agatha scoffed, producing from her handbag a vicious-looking pair of wire cutters. She quickly snipped a new hole in the fence and they wriggled through. They crept forward from tree to tree, then dropped to their hands and knees as they approached the edge of the copse. Lying on their bellies, they had a clear view down into the building compound.

"There are a lot of shipping containers and storage sheds." James was squinting to see clearly, then began fumbling with his binoculars case. "We'll need these to see what's going on." When he looked back, Agatha was already studying the scene through a small but powerful telescope.

"You really did come prepared, didn't you?" he said.

"Tools of the trade," Agatha replied. "Look—there's a huge truck arriving."

An enormous articulated lorry that seemed to fill the narrow lane beyond the compound pulled up at the main gates, which were hauled open by two men. They were swiftly swung closed again after the lorry, hauling a trailer bearing a transport container, had reversed slowly into the compound. There was a flurry of activity, and a large fork-lift appeared from one of the buildings, preparing to unload from the container. What they saw next shocked them both. As the forklift eased a large cage out of the container, there was a flash of something orange and a roar that shook the trees.

"Did I just see what I think I saw?" James whispered.

"You did if you think you saw a tiger," Agatha replied, reaching for her phone. "There's no way anyone should be keeping a tiger in a dump like that!"

"I can see a car arriving," James reported, focusing his binoculars. "The driver has got out and opened one of the rear doors for a man with a beard."

"Keep an eye on them," she said, then concentrated on the phone. "Bill? Listen, you're not going to believe this, but . . ."

She gave Bill Wong a brief run-down of their situation, then held the telescope to her eye again. "I can't see the licence plates on the truck," she told him, "but a black Mercedes just showed up and I can see those plates."

She recited the licence number, then waited for a response. When Bill came back on the line, he sounded gravely concerned.

"Agatha, you and James are to stay out of sight," he said.

"The car is known to be used by a Romanian gangster called Valeriu Fieraru. They call him Barbaneagra—Blackbeard."

"I think he's here," Agatha confirmed.

"Don't let any of them see you," Bill warned. "Especially him. He's dangerous. There's a warrant out for his arrest. The National Wildlife Crime Unit and the National Crime Agency are after him. We'll be there as soon as we can. Don't do anything silly."

"Of course not," she said. "Just get here fast!"

Agatha and James watched and waited for the next forty-five minutes as cages and crates of various sizes were unloaded and spirited away out of sight. They could see nothing more of the cargo's contents, although each item was handled with great care. Agatha fidgeted and grumbled, becoming ever more impatient as time wore on.

"Where are Bill and his lot?" she moaned, shoving her telescope back into her handbag and propping herself on one elbow to turn to James. "Blackbeard will be gone before the police get here."

"I think they may have finished unloading." James was still concentrating on his binoculars.

"Then we need to get back to Eric's place." Agatha raised herself to a crouched position. "Come on, James!"

Once through the fence, they raced back to the forest and had time for only a breathless few words with Eric before they took off in Agatha's car.

"If Blackbeard and his crew are getting ready to leave, we need to delay them," said Agatha, hurling the car round a corner that would take them into the lane leading to the compound.

"So what's the plan?" asked James.

"I was hoping you might come up with something."

"Then you'd better slow down," said James nervously. "I can't think at this speed."

"I've got an idea." Agatha slammed on the brakes and the car screeched to a halt. The lane was barely wide enough for two vehicles to pass, but judging by the way it was hemmed in by tall hedgerows and tree branches creating a canopy above the road, it seldom saw much traffic. "Keep your eyes peeled for anyone coming."

They got out, and James paced backwards and forwards, scanning the road in both directions for any signs of approaching vehicles, while from the other side of the car came a rustle of cloth and the zing of zippers.

"Okay, how do I look?" Agatha asked.

"Wow! That was a quick change!" James was amazed to see her no longer clad in muddied black clothes but in an immaculate short-sleeved powder-blue dress and dark blue suede high heels. "You look amazing."

"Good," she said. "Let's get going again."

The lane twisted through a series of bends that made Agatha marvel at how such a large lorry had managed to negotiate them, then they were suddenly at the compound. Once again, two men were heaving the gates open, and twenty yards away, near the cab of the truck, Blackbeard stood by the Mercedes, preparing to leave. He glowered at Agatha's car as she pulled up across the gateway, blocking any exit. Both the men on the gates looked towards him, and he jerked his head to one side, clearly signalling them to get rid of the unwanted visitors. Agatha and James stepped out of the car.

"Good morning," Agatha called cheerily. "I was wondering if I might have a word with whoever's in charge?"

One of the men walked towards her. He was dressed in a black bomber jacket and jeans. His head and face boasted a layer of stubble that was not quite dense enough to hide the ragged edges of the tattoos that rose like blue-black flames from the neck of his T-shirt.

"You get lost," he grunted with a heavy accent.

"No, no, not at all," Agatha responded, adopting her most professional smile. "We're not lost. I simply need to speak to your boss."

"Not here." The man shook his head.

"Yes, I think here will be fine." Agatha nodded, deliberately obtuse and still smiling. "It's this place that I want to talk to him about. Is that him beside the nice Mercedes?" She pointed and waved to Blackbeard. He shouted something unintelligible at the man and strode towards her.

"What are you doing here?" he asked bluntly. His beard was full and bushy, merging almost seamlessly with his crop of wavy black hair. Agatha could never abide men who grew beards. The facial hair always smelled of stale lager and last night's chicken biryani.

"So nice to meet you," she beamed, reaching out to shake hands. He ignored the gesture. "My name is Selina Valentino and I run a wholesale perfume business. I was told that

77

many of the farmers around here have storage areas that they rent out."

"Not us," growled Blackbeard. "Now move your car."

"What a shame." Agatha looked deflated. "I'm really desperate, you see. Can't you spare me just a little space? I have half a container of Misty Lilac and Primrose Passion landing from Shanghai in two days, and my usual warehouse has burned down. The nightwatchman was apparently smoking pot. What he didn't realise was that he was sitting on a crate full of fireworks. Next thing he knew, a rocket shot up between his legs. They say that if he'd been sitting a few inches further forward, he'd have got properly high—well, bits of him would have. Please say you can help me out. I can pay you well. I can even pay in advance, if you like."

"Move your car now, or I'll drive that truck over it!" Blackbeard yelled in her face, his dark eyes flashing malice. Then he glanced off to the left where a police van had suddenly appeared at the gates, blue lights flashing. His eyes flicked back to Agatha. "You bitch!" he spat, reaching out to grab her. She shuffled backwards, dodging his lunge, and James inserted himself between them. Blackbeard grappled with him, flinging him to the ground and aiming a kick, but uniformed police were now storming the compound and two burly officers bowled him over, one of them handcuffing his wrists in front of him with practised ease.

"Are you okay, James?" Agatha asked, rushing over to where James had landed in a patch of mud and farmyard slurry. He heaved himself upright, clutching his leg.

"I'm fine," he grimaced, "but I think I may have cracked my torch. Selina Valentino?"

"It was all I could think of at the time."

Scuffles broke out, the police subduing Blackbeard's henchmen in various parts of the compound, and Agatha noted that a number of the officers were armed. Blackbeard cursed as the two officers dragged him to his feet.

"This isn't over!" he snarled at Agatha.

"It is for you," she shrugged.

Staring straight at her, he bared his teeth and drew a finger across his throat.

"That's supposed to frighten me, is it?" she said. "Get a shave, Mr. Barbaneagra. There could be anything living in that rat's nest around your chin."

"Keep a close eye on that one." Bill Wong strode towards them, instructing the two officers holding Blackbeard, then turned to Agatha. "I thought I told you to stay out of sight?"

"We had to stop him from leaving." James jumped to her defence. "Agatha was magnificent."

"Yes," Bill sighed and smiled, "I'll bet she was. Thank you both. You know, of course, that I will need to talk to you later at the station for proper statements?"

"We know the drill," Agatha nodded, "but we need to talk to Eric first to let him know that Aslan and the small wizards are going to be all right."

"Aslan and the . . . what?" Bill looked confused.

"It will all be in the statement," said Agatha.

"Good," said Bill. "I'll be here for a while. We need to secure the scene and wait for the guys from the National—"

There came the sudden revving of an engine, a horrendous crash and the sound of splintering wood as the Land Rover smashed through the wall of a store shed. It shot forward, kicking up a cloud of dust, and roared uphill towards the gate in the chain-link fence. The police officers, already occupied with their prisoners, were powerless to stop it bursting through the fence and heading off up the track.

"Where does that track lead?" asked Bill.

"Into the forest," James explained, fishing a map out of his pocket. "Looks like it branches off all over the place once it's deeper into the trees. There are quite a few exits from the forest onto main roads."

"I'll get our people onto it," said Bill, reaching for his radio. "I got his licence number. We'll catch him."

But they didn't. The Land Rover simply melted into the terrain, one of thousands of similar green Land Rovers abroad in the English countryside.

Despite having called ahead to update the team in her office, Agatha was surprised by her welcome when she arrived back at Raisin Investigations following a long afternoon of questions and form-filling at Mircester Police Station. The assembled staff of Toni, Patrick and Helen gave her a loud cheer and a round of applause.

"Fantastic!" Toni grinned. "That must be Raisin Investigations' fastest ever case—from client interview to the arrest of the culprits in less than twenty-four hours!"

"A good result," Agatha agreed, dropping her handbag on Simon's desk and taking his seat. "Not so good if we had been charging by the hour, of course." She smiled, then added, "Which reminds me. Toni, can you run a client check on Eric, just to . . ."

". . . make sure we're not going to charge him a fee he can't really afford." Toni finished Agatha's sentence for her while making a note on a pad. "I'm on it."

"Good," said Agatha. "And where's Simon?"

"He's out on a bin lorry," said Helen, handing Agatha a cup of tea. "They were in our street this morning and he looked like he was having the time of his life. I saw him chatting up housewives and whistling at girls on their way to work."

"I'll tell him to watch his step," Patrick said, shaking his head earnestly. "We don't want him getting sacked because someone's complained about him."

"Sounds like he's getting into the role," Agatha said. "Toni, did you check Simon's notes about Deirdre Higginbotham and where she might be appearing next?"

"I've got her usual schedule here." Toni held up her notepad.

"Good." Agatha took a sip of tea. "Let's talk later. You and I may be able to take that case forward. Patrick, what about the background check on the Admiral?"

"I'm waiting for a few responses from various people," Patrick replied, "but it's shaping up to be an interesting report. I'll have it ready for you first thing tomorrow. I thought we were going to wait until after the coroner's inquest before we started looking into him."

"The inquest is tomorrow morning," Agatha pointed out. "I want to be fully briefed on him before I sit through that. I need to know who he was and what sort of person he was in order to make sense of whatever is said at the inquest."

"Of course," said Patrick, reaching for the phone on his desk. "I'll get right back onto it."

"Thank you for the tea, Helen." Agatha picked up the mug and her handbag, heading for her office. "I'll enjoy it in here while I sort through whatever paperwork awaits."

She settled into her high-backed leather chair, draped her arms across the armrests and leaned back, staring into the distance. It had been a very tedious and exhausting afternoon, but an incredibly exciting, exhilarating morning. Poor James, she chuckled to herself. He couldn't possibly have known what he was letting himself in for. On the other hand, there were very few people who knew her better, so maybe, given everything that had happened since the previous evening, he hadn't exactly been expecting a normal Thursday. He'd put himself in danger when that thug Blackbeard had gone for her. Suddenly her mind was filled with the image of the Romanian's cruel sneer and him dragging his finger across his throat. She shuddered, feeling a sudden chill, and reached for her tea.

The lighting in Le Cheval Blanc in Mircester was soothingly subdued, making it difficult to pick out any details on the labels of the bottles of their most prestigious wines that stood on occasional shelves here and there on the bistro's white walls. Like the lighting, the music was also soft, just loud enough to cover the voices from adjacent tables and keep your own conversation as private as you wanted.

Agatha, still in her powder-blue dress, had been first to arrive and gave Alice Peters a welcoming smile as she settled into the seat opposite. She judged Alice to be elegantly dressed, in a simple white V-neck T-shirt and black jeans. A delicate gold flower pendant hung round her neck on a gold chain.

"That's a pretty necklace," Agatha complimented her.

"A present from Bill." Alice seemed to glow with pride. "I hear you've had another eventful day."

"Well, I wouldn't ever want to let life get boring," Agatha laughed.

Alice raised her glass with a smile and Agatha clinked hers against it. "Here's to Raisin Investigations."

"And here's to Eric Collins," Agatha added. "You can be so wrong about people, can't you? I dismissed the poor man as a crank, but he turned out to be a lovely person. He's delighted that the RSPCA and one of our local wildlife groups are taking care of Joey and using his garden as a base to search for the quokkas that are still out there. He told me his children and grandchildren are arriving en masse at the weekend to go searching for the 'smiley wallababies.'"

"There are still a few on the loose, then?"

"Only a handful, but they need to be found. They're fine in this summer weather, but when it turns colder, they might not survive."

"The kids aren't likely to come across any white lions or tigers, are they?"

"No. All but those quokkas are accounted for. Bill says that Blackbeard's crew kept a pretty good inventory. I'm afraid I added to his workload a bit today."

"He's not bothered about that," Alice said. "He's made some new contacts with the wildlife unit and the National Crime Agency, so he's happy."

"But you're not, are you? Have you told him how upset you are about his parents?"

"Not exactly, but I think he realises what the problem is."

"Does he? He adores them so much that he's blind to their failings. I've seen this happen before. His parents have driven other girls away."

"Other girls? Well, I know I'm not exactly his first girlfriend . . . I'm not even his first fiancée . . ."

"You're not, but are you the one who's going to last the course?"

"I hope so."

"Have you had his mum's Sunday lunch?"

"The canned tomato soup . . ."

"The soggy roast potatoes . . ."

"Beef like grey leather . . ."

"Disintegrating sprouts . . ."

"His mother never took her eyes off me, so I ended up eating the lot." Alice burst out laughing. "It was really awful, but I finished every last mouthful."

"That shows true dedication." Agatha smiled. "You must really love him."

"I do. I really do." Alice sighed. "I can't imagine life without him. I want to spend my whole life with him, but . . ."

"But his mother's cooking is abysmal," said Agatha, taking a sip of wine, "and talking at the table is forbidden."

"That's just as well," Alice groaned, "because all they ever do is tell me how I need to eat more to 'put some meat on your bones, girl!' But I can't do that. I can't put on weight. I'm not like you."

"What does that mean?" Agatha bristled slightly.

"I mean I've never had a great figure like you." Alice swallowed some wine. "I've always been too tall and too skinny with scrawny chicken legs."

"What are you talking about?" Agatha was appalled at her companion's lack of confidence. "You look fantastic. Most women would kill to be able to eat whatever they like and look like you do. You are *so* beautiful—and I know Bill thinks so too."

"Bill always makes me feel special," Alice admitted, and Agatha noted the way her expression softened when she spoke about her fiancé.

"He's grown into a handsome young man," said Agatha. "You two look really glamorous together."

"I don't think his parents agree. I overheard his father telling his mother that he wished Bill would find a nice Chinese girl to settle down with."

"Really?" Agatha paused, wondering for a moment if that was perhaps something Bill's father had *meant* Alice to hear. She had heard him say the same thing about Bill's previous girlfriends. A waiter appeared and topped up her

85

glass from the bottle of Chablis chilling in the ice bucket standing by their table. "You have to try not to take that to heart. Bill's father has been deluding himself for years. He still seems to think that Bill will one day give up being a police officer and join him in his dry-cleaning business."

"That won't happen." Alice shook her head. "Bill loves the job. So do I, for that matter."

"And you are both very good at it," Agatha pointed out, picking up the menu. "Maybe that's something else Mr. and Mrs. Wong need to appreciate. Come on, let's order some food. All that talk of eating whatever you like has made me hungry!"

Agatha ordered a chicken liver and foie gras parfait followed by a ribeye steak, while Alice went for a salmon and crab salad, with roast venison as her main. Having almost polished off their white wine, they each ordered a glass of Beaujolais to enjoy with their main courses. The waiter, a small, round man who looked like he regularly ate his way through the entire menu, complimented them on their choices and began fawning over Alice in an even more complimentary way, warbling in a heavy French accent that Agatha reckoned to be about as genuine as the dodgy diamond in his ear stud.

"That'll do, Napoleon," she chided. "We're hungry and we'd like to eat tonight, if you don't mind."

The waiter nodded with a poorly pronounced "*Mais oui,*" and waddled off.

"I wish I was as strong and confident as you," said Alice.

"What makes you think you're not? I've seen you at work.

There's no lack of confidence when you're dealing with people then—and I've seen you handle some fairly awkward customers."

"Well, that's all down to the training, really."

"Then maybe you need training in how to deal with Ma and Pa Wong."

"They'd have to start a whole new course at the police college for that. Anyway, what I meant was that I've never been as confident as you are with men."

Agatha tutted, savoured the last of her Chablis and looked Alice straight in the eye. "That's mainly just fake and bluster," she admitted. "I can be every bit as insecure as anyone else. I used to tell people that I thought of men like new shoes. You put up with the pain of the blisters because they look good, but as soon as you get used to them, they're chucked in the back of the cupboard because another pair has caught your eye."

Alice giggled, the chat and the wine having relaxed her to the point where Agatha could see she was having fun. "Have you really had as many men as you have new shoes?"

"Well," Agatha was surprising herself with her own honesty, but carried on regardless, "it's actually a lot easier to pick up new shoes. I haven't always been quite as much in control of my love life as I like people to think. In fact, I could tell you—"

She was saved from making any further personal revelations by the ringing of her mobile phone. She reached for it instinctively, without checking who was calling.

"Aggie—I've caught you at last!" It was Charles.

"Don't call me that." There was a sudden chill in Agatha's voice. "What do you want?"

"Actually, I need to discuss some business." Charles managed to maintain a cheerful tone, despite his frosty reception. "A friend of mine needs your help. It would be ideal if you could meet him here at the house on Saturday. Are you free? I have some other friends arriving for dinner if you would like to join us."

"I don't think dinner is a good idea." Agatha's expression was tense, but her voice was calm. "Can't he come to my office?"

"Well, it's dashed awkward, you know. He'd like to keep things a tad more discreet."

"Very well. If he's at the house on Saturday, I can be there in the afternoon, around two."

"Splendid!" Charles sounded genuinely delighted. "I'm looking forward to seeing you again."

"Goodbye, Charles."

The waiter delivered their starters with a dramatically overstated "*Voilà!*" and Agatha dismissed him with a dark glower.

"A problem?" Alice nodded towards the phone that Agatha was tucking into her handbag.

"No." Agatha let out a long breath, then looked across at Alice and recharged her smile, restoring the genial atmosphere they had both been enjoying. "Just an old blister. Let's eat, I'm starved."

Chapter Five

In fair weather, the main square in the centre of Mircester, with its concrete flower beds and public benches, would have been a pleasant enough place to sit and chat, or enjoy a lunchtime sandwich, had it not been for the forbidding presence of Mircester Town Hall. The building loomed over the square, with dark windows set in featureless brick, and uninspired cement columns supporting a triangular shelter over the gloomy entrance—a Victorian architect's cost-constrained failed attempt to mould an empyrean mock-Greek edifice out of common English clay. Agatha rarely gave the unremarkable building any thought at all, but now, looking up at it, she felt dismayed. How could the town planners in the sixties and seventies have torn down so many fine old buildings to make way for ghastly concrete monstrosities, yet somehow have managed to leave the supremely hideous Mircester Town Hall completely unscathed?

She was standing in the sunshine on the steps leading up to the entrance, scanning the notes that Patrick had prepared for her on the Admiral, more correctly known as

Harold Nelson. She smiled to herself, thinking about military nicknames. James had told her how in his army days tall people were nicknamed Shorty, bald people were called Curly and the most morose characters were dubbed Smiler. Now here was Admiral Nelson. She wondered what rank he had actually achieved during his time in the navy. Patrick was still checking on that.

She was steeling herself for the inevitable drudgery of the coroner's hearing when a large, shabby, billowing and wholly unnecessary raincoat approached, containing Dr. Charles Bunbury.

"Ah, Mrs. Raisin," said the pathologist. "I guessed you would be attending these proceedings—"

"Mrs. Raisin? Mrs. Agatha Raisin?" another voice interrupted, and Agatha turned to see a tall, handsome darkhaired man in a finely tailored charcoal-grey suit stepping towards her with hand outstretched. His eyes were as blue as Burmese sapphires, captivating her to the extent that she accepted his handshake without a word. "I'm John Spinner, the coroner. I'll be presiding over today's hearing. So glad to have the chance to talk to you beforehand. Do you mind, Dr. Bunbury?"

He led Agatha away from the pathologist and into a shadowy corner by the building's entrance, lowering his head as though for a confidential conversation. Agatha judged him to be a couple of years older than herself, or possibly a couple of years younger—it was difficult to tell, even though she regarded herself as something of an expert in assessing a man's age and desirability. He had one of those faces that had probably put the ageing process on hold some time in his early forties; a gift, she observed ruefully, that Mother Nature unfairly bestowed rather more often on men than women.

"Is there something I can help you with?" she asked, feeling her voice squeak a little and inwardly scolding herself for allowing herself to flush like a schoolgirl at being the focus of such a charming man's attention.

"I'm sure we can think of something," he gave her a slightly lopsided grin, "but I think I probably rescued you from Dr. Dreary in the nick of time."

"Well, thanks for that." Agatha laughed awkwardly. "I owe you one."

"I suppose you do—so how about dinner tonight?"

"You don't hang around, do you, Mr. Spinner?"

"Life, as they say, is too short, and I've been reading up on you. You intrigue me."

"You make me sound like some kind of academic research project."

"What I was thinking about was a more practical experience—more hands-on, you might say."

His grin now looked worryingly well practised and had taken on a hard edge that Agatha found slightly disturbing.

"No, I would not say that," she said, backing away from him, her smile having melted into a grimace, "and I think *you've* said enough."

"Actions speak louder than words," he reached out to stroke the side of her face, "and I'm sure you like a bit of action."

"Back off," she warned, slapping his hand away, "and don't ever try to touch me again."

"Think it over," he said, pressing a card into her hand. "Here's my number. Give me a call, but don't leave it too long. A woman your age can't afford to pass up too many opportunities."

"A woman my . . . ?" Agatha inhaled slowly, then stuffed the card into his breast pocket, her eyes wide with outrage. "You're not thinking straight. Must be the bruise on your shin."

"What bru—"

Her right foot shot out, the pointed toe of her crocodile-effect shoe demonstrating that it was just as dangerous as the real thing. Spinner winced and his shoulders stooped. His face was taut with pain and fury, although he resisted the indignity of bending to clutch his leg.

"You shouldn't have done that," he hissed. "I'll make sure you regret it."

"You're filling me up with regrets," Agatha growled at him. "I already regret having met you, I regret having listened to you, and I regret not shoving that card right up—"

"Agatha!" Bill Wong was waving from the foot of the steps. Spinner glanced towards him, shot Agatha a look from eyes now as cold as ice, and skulked off.

"Good morning, Bill," Agatha greeted him as he trotted up the steps. "Nice to see a friendly face."

"Wasn't that the new coroner you were talking to?" Bill asked.

"Yes—what happened to the old one?"

"Retired. Snoozed his way through one too many hearings and was advised to go. The new one's so much better to deal with—full of energy and ideas."

"He's certainly full of something. So how is this hearing going to go, Bill?"

"We expect that he'll agree with our findings—that Harold Nelson's death was accidental. There's no evidence to suggest anything else."

"I was sent this." Agatha produced the typewritten note from her handbag. Bill read it quickly, then gave her a weary look.

"Why didn't you show this to me before now, Agatha?"

"Because it's anonymous and untraceable. It's not hard evidence of anything except that someone knows how to use a typewriter."

"That's certainly how Wilkes will see it."

"Yet there's something fishy about the Admiral's death, Bill. He seems to have been the kind of person people either loved or hated. I think someone may well have hated him enough to kill him, and I simply don't believe he drank weedkiller accidentally."

"Well," Bill sighed and scratched his head, "your instincts have been right before, and I'm not happy about the way we had to rush through our procedures. Wilkes won't like it, but I'll try to have a word with the coroner before the hearing starts. He may insist that we spend more time on the case."

The wood-panelled room where the hearing was to be held was overheated and under-ventilated, and the linoleum on the floor, having recently been polished, caused the chairs to make a screech like a sparrow being strangled every time someone stood up or sat down. Fortunately, there were very few people in attendance. Agatha noticed Charlotte Clark, a reporter from the *Mircester Telegraph*, and a couple of people she recognised from the bowls club, as well as Dr. Bunbury and Bill Wong. A woman wearing a black coat sat alone, and from Patrick's notes, Agatha guessed she was Cathy Nelson, the Admiral's widow. She also identified a well-built man and a woman, dressed in white shirts and dark trousers, as the security stewards. At the front of the room, facing the rows of mainly empty chairs, the coroner's clerk, a small, balding man, sat at a desk with a computer terminal. A larger desk, clearly for the coroner himself, took centre stage.

John Spinner marched in carrying a sheaf of papers and barked at the clerk to open a window or two. His icy blue eyes settled on Agatha. "Something in here," he said, "has turned the air foul."

Agatha cocked her head and smiled at him, leaving him in no doubt about who had come off better from their earlier encounter.

Spinner made some introductory remarks and then called on Dr. Bunbury to answer a few questions. Bunbury's answers were long and rambling, the pathologist clearly revelling in the opportunity to show off his knowledge of medical science.

"So, Doctor," Spinner interrupted with exquisite timing, cutting off the monologue during one of the doctor's infrequent pauses for breath, "in short, you believe that the weedkiller was accidentally ingested by the deceased? You believe that he swallowed the stuff when he was in an intoxicated stupor, having drunk a large amount of alcohol on top of having taken a quantity of powerful painkillers?"

"Indeed. The alcohol combined with the painkillers would have left him all but incoherent. Then, given that there are no indications of . . ." Bunbury was clearly gearing up his vocal cords for a fresh oration.

"Yes, we understand," Spinner butted in again. "There is no medical evidence of a struggle or of the deceased being forced to drink the poison. Thank you, Doctor. There is no evidence at all to suggest foul play save for a note of dubious origin presented late in the day to the police by an individual whose motives are decidedly suspect and whose credibility as a witness is questionable, given her past record of abusing this office for her own egotistical personal publicity and pompous self-aggrandisement—"

"That is outrageous!" Agatha leapt to her feet. "How dare you!"

"Ah, it's Mrs. Raisin, isn't it?" Spinner acted as though they had never met. "The previous coroner was once obliged to have you removed from this room. Sit down or I shall do likewise."

"You have no right to question my motives and reputation like that!" Agatha was furious.

"Stewards." Spinner's voice and expression were impassive but his eyes were blue flames of triumph. "Remove this woman from the building."

"Don't worry, I'm going!" Agatha yelled. "But the death of Harold Nelson was no accident! It was murder, and I'm going to prove it!"

All heads were now turned to face her, but the look that drew her eyes like a magnet was not the sneer of John Spinner, the delight of Charlotte Clark or the despair of Bill Wong; it was the haunting expression of Cathy Nelson. She may have been dressed in black, assuming the appearance of a widow in mourning, but despite the fact that she had just listened to distressing evidence about her husband's traumatic final moments, she didn't seem at all distraught. She looked unsettled, possibly a little anxious, but in no way upset. There was not a tear in her eye, and her countenance gave Agatha the distinct impression that none had been shed over the death of Harold Nelson. The grieving widow was devoid of grief.

Charlotte Clark reached Agatha's side before the stewards could close in on her. She had a small digital recorder in her hand.

"So you believe that Harold Nelson was murdered, Mrs. Raisin?"

"I most certainly do," Agatha confirmed, eyeing the stewards. "Let's talk outside, Charlotte."

They sat together in the square, Charlotte holding her recorder in one hand and balancing a notepad on her lap. She used the blunt end of her pencil to stop her glasses slipping down her nose. The glasses were large, with a bright orange and blue design on the frames. Agatha marvelled at the way young people regarded spectacles as a fashion accessory. The journalist was, she guessed, around thirty years younger than her, and when Agatha had been that age, wearing glasses was decidedly unfashionable. She was thankful she had never needed to do so, and even now, when she occasionally used reading glasses to see the tiny print on a bottle of nail varnish, she made sure it was only in the privacy of her own bedroom. Not using the glasses in public had led to the purchase of a few suspect colours, but she regarded that as being a gamble worth taking.

"What makes you think this was murder, Mrs. Raisin?" the younger woman asked.

"I received an anonymous tip-off," Agatha explained, adopting a tone she considered suitable for a press interview, "and my initial enquiries have led me to believe there are grounds for further investigation."

"It doesn't sound like you have very much to go on." Charlotte sounded disappointed. "My editor's not going to see much of a story in this."

"Then pep it up a bit, Charlotte," Agatha suggested. "Use a bit of background from previous cases. If you can get me into the paper, it will encourage people to come forward. Help me out here, and in return . . ."

"An exclusive?"

"You'll get the full story when it's all over—every juicy detail."

Agatha made her way back to her office, her chat with the young reporter bringing back memories of her time as a PR consultant in London. Then, she had played reporters, editors and feature writers off against one another with Machiavellian skill over expense-account lunches that drifted late into the afternoon on a tide of champagne and fine wine. That thought, in turn, gave her a gem of an idea. She wanted someone on the inside at Mircester Crown Green Bowling Club to find out what the members were saying about the Admiral's death. She was known to the people at the club, as was Toni and, in all likelihood, Patrick, so they couldn't go undercover. Simon was busy on the bins, but there was one person she knew who loved sniffing around a murder investigation, who loved listening to gossip, and who loved dressing up. Yes, she knew just the man for the job.

Settling at her desk, she dropped her handbag into its usual drawer, gratefully accepted the cup of coffee Helen offered her, pushed the latest tranche of paperwork aside and picked up her phone.

"It's me," she announced when her call was answered after four rings. "Are you in this neck of the woods again this weekend?"

"Aggie, darling!" She imagined Roy Silver rocking back in his office chair and swinging his Italian leather loafers onto his desk. Once an employee at Agatha's London PR agency, Roy was now a highly successful PR guru in his own right, thanks in no small part to his old boss. "How sweet of you to call. I was thinking about you only this morning when I was having a coffee at Gino's—you remember Gino? He does simply the most gorgeous buttery croissants. Anyway, I was sitting there minding my own business—you know me, never one to eavesdrop on someone else's conversation—when who do you think sat down at the table next to mine? Go on—you'll never guess!"

"Then I'm not even going to try, Roy. Listen, are you up in Blockley riding at Tamara's stables this weekend? I need your help."

"I'm up there most weekends, sweetie," Roy admitted. "Sadly, I don't always have time to drop in for a glass of bubbly with you. What is it that you need help with? It's . . . it's not another lovely murder, is it?"

"That's exactly what it is, Roy. I've got an undercover assignment for you."

"Undercover . . . ?" Agatha heard Roy take a sharp breath and could sense him fanning himself with a flat hand. "You can rely on me. I'm cancelling everything. I'll be at your place later this evening. Fill me in then. Must dash."

With that, he hung up, and Agatha knew he would be rushing home to pack an array of outfits to cover every conceivable eventuality, although she was reasonably confident that Roy's famously extensive wardrobe would not include bowling whites. Those he would be able to pick up in Mircester, and the shopping trip would only add to his excitement.

"You look very pleased with yourself." Toni stood in the doorway, smiling at Agatha's self-satisfied expression.

"I am. I've just recruited Roy to do some digging for us at the bowls club."

"He'll love that." Toni laughed. "White trousers, white shoes, a nice blazer—he'll be in seventh heaven."

"No doubt," Agatha agreed. "He'll have to sign up as a novice, though. I doubt he's ever been bowling before."

"He'll pick it up," said Toni, then tapped her watch. "We need to leave shortly."

"Ah, yes." Agatha reached down to retrieve her handbag. "Miss Higginbotham's early-afternoon appearance at Shirley's Girlies. We wouldn't want to miss that, would we?"

Shirley's Girlies was tucked away amongst a dingy tangle of shops and warehouse premises beyond Mircester's railway station. It was a part of town Agatha knew existed but had seldom had any reason to visit. Even when she took the train into London, she preferred to use the station at Moreton-in-Marsh, which was easier for her to reach from Carsely. The street had a corner pub called The Sportsman offering "Live TV Sport All Day," shops that boasted they were "House Clearance Specialists" with second-hand fridges and washing machines sitting outside on the pavement, and places where only plumbers or electricians could possibly understand what was for sale.

In the brick arches supporting the railway line, there were gloomy auto repair workshops run by the sort of mechanics who would fix the problem with your car then suck air through their teeth while pointing out two or three other things that also needed urgent attention, and which doubled the bill. They all appeared to know a place where they could buy pre-stained overalls with casual rips, and they had an inexhaustible supply of rags that they seemed to use for wiping oily grease *onto* their hands.

Shirley's Girlies had, without doubt, the brightest frontage of any of the premises in the street. Neon lights were bent into the shape of dancing girls who kicked and twisted as the light flicked from red to blue and back again. Agatha parked her car a discreet distance from the club, and Toni, aiming her camera's powerful telephoto lens, tried in vain to capture an image of Deirdre Higginbotham disappearing down the shadowy alleyway to the left of the main entrance.

"With her hood up and her head down, we'll never get a decent shot of her," Agatha said, reaching over to retrieve a neat black briefcase from the back seat of the car. "We need to get inside. Okay, our story is that we're from a talent agency and we want to see the owner. With any luck, we can talk Shirley—if that's her real name—into thinking we might have clients she would be interested in and push her into discussing who she employs as dancers. At the very least, we'll get a look at the place without arousing suspicion."

They approached the main entrance, where a large man in a dark coat stood guard, nodding to regular patrons as they slipped inside.

"Good afternoon," said Agatha brightly. "We're from the Starry Eyes talent agency and we'd like to talk to the owner."

The man grunted, produced a small walkie-talkie from

his pocket and mumbled into it. The response came via an earpiece and was inaudible to Agatha and Toni. The man nodded, said, "No, just two women," then nodded again.

"You can go in," he told them, pushing open the door. "Shirley will see you. Wait in reception."

The reception area was softly lit, with a dark red carpet and walls painted in a matching tone. The dull, muted thump of music indicated that a performance was under way somewhere deep inside the club. The reception desk doubled as a cloakroom counter; behind it sat a well-endowed young woman with a mane of black and purple hair and make-up that would not have looked out of place in a horror movie. Clearly one of the artistes when not front of house, she was chewing gum and tapping out a text message on her phone.

"Shirley sez wait," she said, looking up slowly, the boredom in her expression deepened by the languor in her eyes.

Agatha and Toni stood primly to one side while a steady trickle of customers filed in, some hurrying silently past and some rolling in merrily, fuelled by a lunchtime session in The Sportsman. Two men then approached from the corridor that led into the main area of the club. One was large and overweight, with the build of a boxer gone to seed, a fuzz of close-cropped grey hair and a nose that might once have been straight many fights ago. The other was just tall enough to reach the bigger man's shoulder and had a rodent-like face. Both wore white shirts, dark sports jackets and jeans.

"Who are you?" the larger man asked, eyeing them suspiciously.

"We're here to see Shirley." Agatha smiled politely.

"I'm Shirley," the man replied with a snort. "Shirley Jenkins. This is my place."

"You're Shir . . . ?" Agatha failed to hide her surprise. "I'm sorry. I was expecting . . ."

"A woman?" Jenkins shook his head with a resigned sigh. "Yeah, I get that a lot. Always have done. Usually I tell people I *am* a woman but the hormone treatment's gone wrong, don't I, Ferret?"

"You do, boss." The man called Ferret laughed enthusiastically. "That's what he usually says all right."

"So who are you?" demanded Jenkins.

"We're from the Starry Eyes talent agency." Agatha switched on a professional smile and reached out to shake hands. Jenkins's massive paw engulfed her hand, but his grip was mercifully gentle. "I'm Anita and this is Sylvia."

"Come through this way, away from the door," Jenkins said, turning to lumber back down the corridor, with Ferret scuttling in his wake. He led them to the performance area, dominated by a brightly lit raised platform that was part stage, part catwalk. In the relative darkness surrounding the stage, men sat at tables, scantily clad waitresses moving swiftly between the bar and their customers carrying trays laden with drinks. The music stopped as they entered the room, and Agatha caught enough of a glimpse of the dancer leaving the stage to discern, by the lack of the relevant tattoo, that she was not Cindy Snakehips. Jenkins ordered mineral water and Agatha and Toni followed suit.

"What's your angle?" Jenkins asked above the hubbub of background conversation. "Some kind of mother-and-daughter act?"

"I'm sorry?" Agatha wasn't quite sure what she had just heard.

"A twosome?" asked Jenkins. "You know, a novelty act. Young Sylvia looks like she should be able to shake it about, but you're a bit long in the tooth."

"A bit what?" Agatha's professional smile was suddenly extinguished. Toni tried to rest a calming hand on her arm, recognising that the cold look settling on Agatha's face in no way reflected the red-hot temperature of the anger that was about to erupt.

"Still, if you want to show me your act, I'm game." Jenkins placed his drink on the bar. "I need to know you ain't past it. You can get your kit off and show me the goods in my office."

"We'll do no such thing!" Agatha roared.

"No?" Jenkins shrugged. "Push off, then. I don't want the punters being put off by having some old tart hanging around."

"Some old . . . ?" Agatha hurled the contents of her glass into Jenkins's face. He spluttered, wiping his eyes with his knuckles, and Ferret took a step towards her. Toni flicked a foot forward to trip him, catching his ankle and sending him stumbling into a waitress, whose tray of drinks went crashing to the floor.

104

"What the hell is your problem?" howled Jenkins, mopping his face with a bar towel.

"Indeed," came a familiar voice. "Just what *is* your problem, Mrs. Raisin?"

To Agatha's horror, the face of DCI Wilkes loomed out of the darkness. With him was a man Agatha vaguely recognised as another detective. The second man held a small wallet open in front of Jenkins, identifying himself as a police officer.

"Wilkes." She scowled at him. "Why am I not surprised to see you in a place like this?"

"While I *am* rather surprised to see you," he said, before draining the whisky glass in his hand and placing it on the bar. "And appalled to witness you and your associate assaulting these two gentlemen."

"You don't know what you're talking about!" Agatha pointed a finger at Wilkes's face. He smiled and with one swift movement snapped a handcuff on her wrist. When she squealed and reached for the cuff with her free hand, he cuffed that one too.

"Agatha Raisin," he sneered, "you're under arrest."

"You can't do this!" Agatha shrieked.

"I just have," Wilkes chuckled. "I can hardly believe we came in here to meet a couple of contacts and ended up hitting the jackpot. You'll be formally detained and charged down at the station."

Toni shot a look towards the entrance, seeking out an escape route, but saw the doorman closing on her from that direction, then glanced back to see Wilkes's sidekick shaking his head at her. She had nowhere to run, so held her hands out in front of her and watched the detective cuff her wrists too.

The only thing to mitigate the ignominy of being led out of an establishment like Shirley's Girlies in handcuffs and being bundled into the back of a police car, albeit an unmarked one, was that no one known to either Agatha or Toni was likely to have seen them in that particular club, in that particular street, in that particular area of Mircester. With Wilkes at the wheel, laughing heartily, revelling in the fact that he had handcuffed the high-and-mighty Agatha Raisin, Agatha leant towards Toni and whispered, "Say nothing."

Mircester Police Station was but a short drive away, and the custody sergeant looked up from his desk as Wilkes marched his prisoners in.

"Aha, DCI Wilkes," he greeted them. "I've just had a Mr. Shirley Jenkins on the phone saying that he won't be pressing charges against these ladies. He doesn't want any fuss. I suspect he doesn't want his punters to think there are police officers lurking in his club."

"What a shame." Wilkes pulled a mock-sad face. "Yet after what I witnessed earlier, I feel obliged to—"

"You're not obliged to do anything further," Agatha interrupted quickly. "You failed to caution or arrest us properly at the club and you have driven us here in an official police vehicle after you've been drinking alcohol. I saw you downing what looked like a double, and the car stank of cheap whisky. If you are convicted of driving under the influence

106

in an official car, you'll likely lose your job and your pension. How many did you have in the club, Wilkes? Should I insist that the sergeant breathalyses you, or would you rather . . . ?" She held up her hands, indicating the cuffs.

Wilkes paused for a moment, started to object, then shrugged his shoulders, sighed and reached into his pocket for the handcuff keys.

Having taken a taxi back to her car with Toni, Agatha let out a long breath as she pulled out of their parking space and drove off past The Sportsman.

"Well," she said, looking across at her assistant. "This afternoon didn't go entirely according to plan. I feel I should apologise for landing you—"

"No need," said Toni, and burst out laughing. "Where else could I get a job like this? After everything we've been through together, I don't think I could cope with, say, being the receptionist at Shirley's Girlies, do you?"

"No," Agatha smiled, "and you'd look awful with purple hair!"

"You know," Toni said, sounding more serious, "that thing about mother and daughter . . . well, I'd be proud for anyone to think of me as your daughter and you as . . ." She saw the look of growing alarm on Agatha's face and stumbled over her words. "But of course you don't look nearly old enough, so no one would ever . . . I mean, it would be . . . I'll stop talking now."

They drove the rest of the way in silence. When they

arrived back at the office, Patrick was at his desk, his phone clamped to his ear and his free hand making notes on a pad. Helen swung into action to provide everyone with tea and chocolate digestives, although Agatha declined the latter, and by the time she was sitting in her office with Toni, taking their first sips, Patrick was eager to talk.

"I've been able to track down quite a bit on Harold Nelson. He was born in Mircester in 1936 and left school at the age of fifteen, although he doesn't seem to have spent too much time there anyway. He joined the Royal Navy as a boy seaman and was posted to HMS Ganges—that's a shore station near Ipswich, not a ship—for training. After a year there, he went to sea, but he seems to have been back in Mircester whenever he got the chance. He was arrested for drunk and disorderly a few times, and in 1956 he married a local girl, Constance Fairweather. No record of any children, and she died three years later when she fell out of a window. She was pregnant at the time."

"That's awful," said Toni. "He must have been devastated."

"Hard to tell," said Patrick. "He went straight back to the navy. He was certainly no admiral, though. He spent years shovelling coal into boilers on the old steamships and never progressed much beyond the lower ranks. He had a problem with discipline—generally to do with being drunk.

"Despite that, he spent twenty-two years in the navy. When he came out, he was still a relatively young man, and he spent the next twenty-five years or so as a merchant seaman. He returned to Mircester when he eventually retired twenty years ago. Seven years ago, aged seventy-eight, he married his second wife, Catherine, known as Cathy, who is twenty years his junior."

"I saw her at the coroner's inquest," said Agatha. "She didn't seem too upset about the passing of her husband. We need to talk to Mrs. Cathy Nelson, Toni."

"Already on it," Toni confirmed. "She's agreed to see us tomorrow morning. She seemed quite keen when I spoke to her on the phone."

"Really?" Agatha was surprised. "That's not the reaction one would expect from a grieving widow. That, I'm sure, will be an interesting meeting. In the meantime, I have something else I need you both to do, but you are absolutely sworn to secrecy."

"Naturally," said Patrick. "Everything we do at Raisin Investigations is strictly confidential."

"This isn't really for the company," Agatha explained. "It's kind of personal and involves a close friend—someone who's a friend to all of us."

"It's not the thing with Sir Charles's friend, is it?" Toni asked, reaching into her handbag to arm herself with a note-pad and pen.

"No, I'll deal with that myself," said Agatha. "What I need you to do is to dig up all the background you can get on this couple." She slid a piece of paper across the desk. On it were two names.

"Really?" Toni couldn't hide her surprise. "You want us to investigate Bill Wong's parents?"

"Not investigate exactly," Agatha said. "I just need to

know more about their past, their family history, where they've lived, what jobs they've had, that sort of thing."

"Digging up info on Bill's family doesn't feel right," Toni said. "Are we allowed to ask why?"

"I'd rather not say," Agatha said, "but it's nothing sinister. Just a favour to help make Bill's life a little easier. So, Patrick, you once spent some time on some sort of exchange thing with the Hong Kong Police, didn't you?"

"That was a lot of years ago." Patrick seemed impressed that Agatha had remembered that detail about his police service. "Most of my contacts there are long since retired, but I daresay they will still know people who know people . . ."

"Good." Agatha nodded. "I was hoping you'd say that. Toni, you're a local girl and so is Mrs. Wong. See if you can find someone who knew her way back when she got married to Bill's father. And we need to keep this discreet, okay? Totally hush-hush. I don't want any of it getting back to Bill or his parents."

"You haven't mentioned Alice once," said Toni, toying with her pen. "This is about her and Bill, isn't it?"

"Clever girl," Agatha nodded, "but that stays between us three. We have a chance to help them out of a messy situation, but . . ."

". . . but if Bill or his parents find out, then the whatsit will really hit the fan," finished Patrick.

"Precisely," Agatha agreed. "So tread carefully. Now, I need to get on with making a few notes for another favour—one I promised Mrs. Bloxby I'd do tonight."

Patrick returned to his desk and Toni was following him

out of the door when Agatha looked up from the notes she had already started scribbling.

"Oh, and Toni . . ." she called.

"Yes?"

"I'd be proud, too."

They exchanged a brief smile and a nod, then carried on as if nothing had happened.

Chapter Six

"But you're not actually a real detective, are you?" Like so many of the other women in the room, this one was wearing her coat indoors, even though St. Jude's church hall was pleasantly warm. From where she was standing behind a lectern at the front of the hall, Agatha could see that the woman was in fact sitting in the middle of a row of half a dozen similar women, all wearing their coats, all of a certain age, all very well upholstered and all frozen in exactly the same pose, their hands folded in their laps, protectively covering their handbags. Who on earth did they think was going to mug them for their pension books and pocket-sized tissue packs in a church hall?

There's always one, Agatha thought to herself. Always one who wants to show off, to be the centre of attention, to let everyone know how clever she is. Then she shook her head, uncomfortably aware that she'd been described that way herself more than once. Well, that gave her an advantage. She knew how to handle this old trout.

"I think that, had you been listening to my talk over the

past hour, my record as a detective, especially when it comes to tracking down murderers, speaks for itself." Agatha had agreed at short notice to present a talk about investigating murder to a combined audience of Carsely and Mircester ladies' societies as a favour to Mrs. Bloxby following a cancellation by her scheduled speaker, a beekeeper from Bicester who claimed never to have been stung in more than forty years tending bees. Then she was, on the ear, and suffered a bizarre allergic reaction, causing her ear to swell up to elephantine proportions, making it impossible for her to wear her glasses.

"But you've had no proper training, have you?" The woman was persistent.

"Do you mean like a police detective?" Agatha asked. This woman was annoyingly familiar and a nagging thought was flashing like a red light bulb at the back of her mind, yet she couldn't place her. She was certainly part of the Mircester contingent. "I can assure you that not all of them put their training to best use."

"So now you're saying that our police are useless?"

"I'm saying nothing of the sort. Most of them are highly skilled and thoroughly professional. I have some very good friends who are police officers and one of my staff at Raisin Investigations is a retired policeman."

"Aha!" the woman crowed triumphantly. "So you rely on his police training to solve your cases. I suspected as much."

"His knowledge and experience are invaluable because—"

"Because you don't actually have any training as an investigator yourself?"

"No, because we need to be able to bring a broad range of talents to bear on a case. I have a great deal of experience in a number of areas that most police officers do not."

"Including being arrested. You've been arrested a few times, haven't you? It was in the papers." The woman turned to her friends sitting either side and nodded smugly.

"The papers also reported the murders I solved." Agatha could feel a tension in her jaw and realised that she was now speaking through gritted teeth. "Despite police ineptitude."

"Good gracious!" The woman made a play of appearing shocked. "Are you really calling our brave British police officers inept?"

"Not all of them, but you have no way of knowing the kind of dirty tricks I've seen some officers pull to cover their blunders in order to save their jobs and pensions."

"I don't think that you, Mrs. Raisin, never having served in uniform, can be expected to appreciate the dedication and sacrifice made by our boys in blue." The woman had clearly now gone into full lecture mode, and Agatha's blood began to boil as she felt herself being scolded like a child. She took a deep breath to calm her temper. She was, after all, in a church hall and doing a favour for her friend, Mrs. Bloxby. "Furthermore," the woman continued, "I think we can well do without the so-called police scandals manufactured by the gutter press. Perhaps we should all be protected from that sort of muck-raking to preserve our respect for the force. Indeed, as the poet Thomas Gray said, 'Where ignorance is bliss, 'tis folly to be wise.'"

Agatha hated people firing arty-farty quotes at her, especially when they came from long-dead poets.

"Well, if ignorance is bliss, you must be as happy as a pig in sh—" She stopped herself just in time.

"Really, Mrs. Raisin. You need to be more tolerant. A good detective would at least try to see things from my point of view!"

That was the final straw.

"Oh, I'm trying all right," Agatha snarled, "but I'm not sure I can get my head that far up my own backside."

"My goodness, is that the time?" Mrs. Bloxby eased Agatha to one side and took her place behind the lectern. "And what a spirited discussion that turned out to be!" Then, facing the woman in the crowd, she added, "You certainly seem very well informed about police matters, Mrs. . . . ?"

"Mrs. Wilkes." The woman nodded with an ungracious smile. "My son is a very important, very respectable police officer."

"Your son is DCI Wilkes!" The nagging red light bulb exploded.

"He is indeed," said the woman, swelling with pride.

"Respectable? Really?" Agatha scoffed. "Ask him what he was doing drinking whisky this afternoon in Shirley's Girlies strip club in Mircester—and yes, before you ask, I *do* have a witness who can corroborate that statement!"

The woman's mouth opened and closed like an old trout now stranded, and a murmur of laughter rolled around the audience. To her left and right, Mrs. Wilkes's posse each briefly removed one hand from their handbags in order to cover smiles or sniggers.

"Well, I'm afraid that's all we have time for this evening." Mrs. Bloxby was keen to bring the meeting to a close. "Thank you all for coming, and a big thank-you to Mrs. Raisin for her fascinating talk."

There was an immediate round of polite applause that lasted for the appropriate length of time before the ladies rose from their seats, some congregating in small groups to chat, others filing out of the hall. Mrs. Wilkes and her group were the first to leave. A few from the audience came forward to shake Agatha's hand and tell her how much they had enjoyed the evening. One, a tall, slim woman who appeared to be in her late seventies but stood upright and unbowed, immaculately dressed in a dark blue overcoat and with not one strand of her solidly permed grey hair out of place, drew Agatha to one side. She introduced herself as Miss Palmer and thanked Agatha for the talk in a way that offered no doubt there was a "but" left hanging in the air. Then it came, her voice lowered to a clandestine level.

"But you did not mention the murder of Harold Nelson."

"Following the coroner's inquest this morning, that is something I'm starting to look into."

"Yet you already knew he was murdered."

"What makes you say that? I had my suspicions, of course, but you seem very interested in this case. Is there something you would like to tell me?"

"I have a great deal to tell you, Mrs. Raisin. I know how

he was murdered, I know why he was murdered and I know who murdered him." Miss Palmer looked from side to side, scanning the room. "But we can't talk here. Come to see me on Sunday, after church." She reeled off her address in Willow Way, and then hurried out of the hall.

Mrs. Bloxby appeared at Agatha's side. "Everything all right, Mrs. Raisin?" she asked.

"Yes, yes, of course," Agatha replied. "I've just had the most extraordinary conversation."

"I saw you talking to Miss Palmer. It all looked very serious."

"So you know her?"

"Yes, she's one of ours, not one of the Mircester lot. 'A spinster of this parish' is how she might be described, although they say she almost got married a few years ago. She was very close to that old chap Mr. Nelson who died at the bowling green."

"He didn't just die," Agatha pointed out. "He was murdered. We're investigating it now."

"Really? Well, I doubt Miss Palmer's involved. She's a gentle soul. She was devastated when Nelson ditched her in order to marry a younger woman."

"Quite remarkable." Agatha shook her head in amazement. "From what I've heard about him, he doesn't seem like the kind of man who would have women competing for his attention. Has Miss Palmer always lived around here?"

"She comes from Mircester originally. She worked for a company there for years before retiring to a cottage on the outskirts of Carsely."

"What did she do?"

"She was a secretary, I believe. Looked after general admin, that sort of thing."

"So she would know how to use a typewriter?"

"Undoubtedly. Most of her working life was way before the computer age."

"Mrs Raisin! How lovely to see you again!" A small elderly woman approached them and it took Agatha a moment to realise who she was.

"Mrs. Swinburn, how are you?" she said, congratulating herself on recognising her. "It's good to see you up and about. You look like you've recovered well from that awful business at the bowls club."

"Oh yes. They didn't keep me in the hospital. I was home that evening, fighting fit again!" The woman smiled and raised a triumphant clenched fist, a gold watch bracelet sliding down her wrinkled wrist. She was wearing too much lipstick and her face was dusted thickly with powder, but the glint in her eyes showed that there was life in the old girl yet. "Anyway, Charlie will be waiting outside, so I must run."

Running, Agatha mused, was undoubtedly something Mrs. Swinburn had not done since she left school, yet she headed for the door with a confident stride.

"She's the one who found the body on the bowling green," Agatha explained.

"That must have been horrid for her." Mrs. Bloxby was genuinely concerned, one of the many virtues that made her so well suited to life as a vicar's wife. Agatha marvelled

118

at how this fundamentally good-natured woman could always find a small place in her heart for anyone who needed a kind thought or sympathetic prayer. Although they were firm friends, it was a trait that regularly made Agatha feel somewhat inadequate.

"I'll get over it," she muttered. "I mean . . . um . . . she seems to have got over it, doesn't she? Can I just ask . . . what time does church finish on Sunday morning?"

"I take it you're not considering attending?" Mrs. Bloxby smiled with raised eyebrows. "Otherwise you would have asked what time church *started* on Sunday."

"I'm afraid your husband might die of shock if he saw me sitting in one of his pews," Agatha laughed. "Miss Palmer wants to meet me after church."

"You may be right about Alf." Mrs. Bloxby chuckled. "He sometimes runs over, but the service starts early and usually ends about ten thirty."

Agatha said her goodbyes and headed home, leaving Mrs. Bloxby to organise the stacking of chairs and the sweeping of the floor. Once the hall was cleared, she had more stacking to do, this time in the dishwasher, taking care of the cups, saucers, plates and cutlery that had been used for the tea and cake before the talk, the two ladies' societies clearly having competed to outdo each other in the Victoria sponge stakes.

"Is it safe?" Alf Bloxby poked his head round the kitchen door.

"Yes, they've all gone." Mrs. Bloxby laughed. "You can come out of your study. Would you like some cake?"

"That would be splendid," Alf said, with genuine enthusiasm. He knew that all the sponges, along with their jam fillings, would be home-made to a scrumptious standard, such was the pride of the women involved. "It's not that I didn't want to meet them, but I was very busy with paperwork. I will admit, however, that a hall full of women with that dreadful Mrs. Raisin at their head is a daunting prospect. Anything might happen if she got them riled up—insurrection, revolution, anything."

"Mrs. Raisin is nowhere near as frightening as you seem to think," she smiled, handing her husband a large slice of cake, "and she was a big help to you when that poor curate was murdered. She got you off the hook."

"That was a terrible time," Alf admitted, disappearing with the cake back in the direction of his study, "and I was thankful. Yet she is a dangerous person to be around. Murder follows in her footsteps."

"Quite the reverse actually, my dear," Mrs. Bloxby said softly, mainly to herself. "She stalks the perpetrators of murder, and they *are* truly dangerous people. Stay safe, Agatha. I will pray for you."

The following morning, Agatha rose early, slipped into a dressing gown and made her way downstairs. Boswell and Hodge wound themselves around her legs, threatening to trip her in a desperate bid for breakfast.

"You can't be this hungry again," she reasoned with them. "I gave you huge portions when I got home last night." The cats, whom she often suspected could understand every word she said, simply stared up at her with big eyes, feigning ignorance.

She made her way to the kitchen, filled their bowls to a chorus of delighted meows and purrs, then opened a window to dispel the smell of cat food. She picked up the container from the previous evening's chicken tikka ready meal, which she had nuked in the microwave the moment she arrived back from the church hall, and dropped it in the bin. James had been in London, being wined and dined by his publisher, and a microwave supper was all she had the energy for. Yesterday had been pretty full-on. The tidying-up had been forgotten when a couple of glasses of Shiraz had made a TV documentary about the successful reintroduction of the red kite to the wild in Britain seem unmissable.

Then Roy had arrived, struggling under the weight of a mountain of suitcases. He had demanded to be brought right up to date on the investigation, and thankfully that hadn't taken too long, because he had already read about the body on the bowling green. His excitement had been infectious, giving Agatha a second wind that had carried her through to the wee small hours, chatting and reminiscing with him. She assumed he was still upstairs in her spare bedroom. She hadn't bothered checking.

Reaching for the coffee pot, she debated whether to go for instant and then had the sudden feeling that something was missing. She looked round at the worktops, the hob and the kitchen table. She couldn't quite put her finger on it. What was it that wasn't there? Then it came to her. Not so long ago, her breakfast would have consisted of two cups of strong coffee and four cigarettes. Now there was no lighter, no ashtray and no packet of king-size filter tips. Smoking was now so much in her past that she had almost forgotten about the old addiction.

"Well, I don't need those things any more, do I, boys?" She grinned at the cats and fancied, quite without foundation, that they grinned back. Her phone rang and she snatched it off the table. Maybe it was James. She hoped it was, but she didn't recognise the number on the screen.

"Hello?"

"Good morning. Am I talking to Mrs. Agatha Raisin?"

"Who wants to know?"

"Can I check that we have the right address here—Lilac Lane in Carsely?"

"Why?"

"According to our records, you have recently been involved in an accident and—"

"Bugger off." Agatha hung up. It was the sixth such speculative call she'd had that week. Somehow she had managed to get on someone's cold-calling list. An accident? She hadn't had an accident, but what if she had? How could these people go fishing like that, cynically trying to take advantage of someone who might have gone through a huge trauma—promising to win them a huge compensation package and cutting a fat chunk out of it for themselves? What gave them the right to go poking their noses into other people's business? On the other hand, wasn't that

122

just what she did herself? Prying into people's private lives? Was she really any better than the cold caller?

Yes, she decided with a firm nod, of course you are! You are Agatha Raisin of Raisin Investigations, and what you do matters. You change people's lives for the better and make sure that rogues, scoundrels, even murderers get what's coming to them. You're not a bit like those cold callers. People come to you asking for help, you don't go chasing them. You don't play on people's fears and insecurities, especially after some kind of tragic accident has befallen them, in order to make a quick profit.

"Heartless swine," she sighed to the cats.

"I do hope you don't mean me." James appeared at the open kitchen window, having stepped over the fence from his own back garden next door, holding two steaming mugs. "Coffee?"

"James," she said, pulling her robe tightly closed in a display of modesty that she assumed was probably wasted on him. "I'm not actually dressed yet."

"Don't bother on my account," he said, confirming her assumption and passing her coffee through the open window. "I see you made the paper today."

He produced a copy of the *Mircester Telegraph* opened to page four, where the headline read: *Private Eye Thrown out of Town Hall.*

"The story's a little kinder than the headline," Agatha muttered, scanning the text.

"Editors love inventing headlines." James nodded. "Are you off out today?"

"I'm meeting the Admiral's widow this morning," Agatha said, "then I have a meeting this afternoon at Barfield House."

"With Charles?"

"Yes, with Charles."

"Oh."

"What do you mean, 'Oh'? I thought you two were friends nowadays."

"And I thought you two were not."

"It's purely business. Someone's trying to stitch up a friend of his with a paternity suit and they want me to look into it."

"So Charles calls and you go running?"

"It's not like that at all. I can't just ignore him forever. Look, why don't we try your place in Evesham this evening—the one we never made it to after the quokka incident? My treat."

"I'll see what I can do," James said, and wandered off towards his own garden.

That, Agatha thought, was like a return to the old, cold James. His apparent aloofness had immediately made her want to win him over, just as it always had before, but there was something different in this morning's offhand attitude. He hadn't been disinterested or insular. He had been . . . jealous. She smiled. Poor James. Even when he thought he was being cool, all he was really doing was showing he cared.

"Surprise!" Roy appeared in the kitchen dressed in a white flat cap, white shirt, white windcheater, white flannels and white shoes. He reminded Agatha that she hadn't yet cleaned her teeth. He looked like a squeeze of toothpaste.

"You've already got all the kit! Well done. I thought we'd have to do some emergency shopping to get you what you needed for the bowls club."

"No, I am an accomplished bowler," Roy boasted. "There are hundreds of bowling clubs all over London, you know—it's not just a villagey thing for you lot out here in the sticks. A friend of mine got me into it at a fantastic place down at Parsons Green, near the Hurlingham Club."

"So you not only look the part, but you have some of the skills as well." Agatha smiled. She was genuinely impressed.

"I do," said Roy, unzipping a small brown leather case to show two shiny black bowls. "And this is my ball bag," he added, sniggering.

"Please, Roy." Agatha's smile turned to a warning look of reproach. "No off-colour jokes at the club. I need you to fit in there and get people to trust you, to talk to you. I don't want you putting them off."

"I'll be on my best behaviour, I promise." He held up his free hand to protest his innocence. "I need to get down there now. There are always members hanging around these clubs tending the flower beds or painting the window frames or whatever, and I want to seem keen." With that, he was gone, and the kitchen suddenly seemed a little duller without the whiteness of his presence.

An hour later, Agatha was ready to leave too, having selected a pale yellow cotton midi dress with a pattern of leaves and flowers rising from the hemline not quite as far as the waist. She was pleased with the way it looked, the sleeves dropping halfway down her upper arms, showing off the tan she had managed to acquire from odd moments reading in the garden. They would also keep her a little warmer if necessary, a few clouds having rolled in overnight, perhaps heralding the end of the recent spell of blue-sky weather.

In Mircester, Toni was waiting for her at the end of the street where she lived, as arranged, smartly dressed in a blue jacket and white jeans. She directed Agatha to Mircester Park Road and an apartment block that looked out over the park. The building was five or six storeys in height, with rows of balconies along the front, some of which had privacy surrounds made from the kind of murky opaque glass that looked like it had been dipped in sour milk. Others had railings, behind which were plants in pots, a tatty leather armchair, an old rusting washing machine, and right up on the top floor, Agatha could swear there was a motorbike.

"It's not as pretty as Miss Featherstone's place, is it?" said Toni.

"You mean the Venusian drop-in centre?" Agatha was making her way towards the main entrance down a flight of steps that bridged a grass embankment. "No, it's not."

The entrance hall was clean and serviceable, yet utterly devoid of charm, with a prevalence of grey paint and grey flooring. They made for the elevator, even though the Admiral's apartment was only on the second floor, and waited just a moment for it to arrive, surprisingly silently and efficiently. Mrs. Nelson was waiting for them in the second-floor corridor. She was in her mid sixties, slim, of average height, and her shoulder-length dark hair was streaked with grey.

"Saw you coming in," she said, beckoning them to follow her round a corner. "My place is along here."

She led them into a flat that was dingy and ill-lit, and, in Agatha's opinion, badly needed the attention of a good interior designer. It seemed fairly clean and tidy, but stank of stale cigarette smoke. Agatha shuddered to think that her own cottage might ever have smelled like that, then consoled herself with the reassurance that her cleaner, Doris Simpson, would never have allowed it.

The sitting room was crowded with furniture that was too big for a small flat, the one area of clear floor space being by the sliding glass doors that led out onto the balcony. There stood a telescope mounted on a tripod. Mrs. Nelson saw Agatha eyeing it and snorted.

"That were his, weren't it?" She had a sneer on her face that turned the smoker's wrinkles around her mouth into a cruel scar pattern. "Said he used it to keep an eye on that bowling club of his in the park. More often than not he had it pointing the other way, towards the nurses' flats at Mircester Hospital. Dirty old man."

She reached forward for her cigarettes, which were on the coffee table between her and her visitors, then saw Agatha following her movement. She picked up a magazine and placed it on top of some official-looking documents that were sitting on the table before lighting up.

"Don't mind, do you?" she said, indicating the lit cigarette. "Don't matter if you do anyway. Now Harry's gone, this is my place, ain't it? He liked his rum and I like my smokes. Normally I go out on the balcony, but there ain't room out there for the three of us."

"I'm very sorry about what happened to your husband, Mrs. Nelson." Agatha offered her condolences.

"It were a nasty way to go, right enough," Mrs. Nelson agreed. "I wouldn't have wished that on him."

"But you're glad he's gone," Agatha said.

"I didn't say that."

"No, but it's true, isn't it?"

"I won't miss him. Reckon he got what he deserved."

"You give the impression," said Toni, sounding surprised at Mrs. Nelson's attitude, "that you really didn't like him very much."

"I hated him." The sneer was back on Cathy Nelson's face and she took a long drag on her cigarette. "He was an absolute bastard—but I never killed him."

"Why did you marry him in the first place?" Toni asked.

"Because I was stupid—and because he offered me something I've never had. A proper home." She waved an arm around the room. "This place. Oh, and he could be a real charmer when he wanted to. Told me he would look after me, that he would take care of me. Said he were a retired admiral. He said that to a lot of people—what a liar. Do you know what a retired admiral's pension is? I do—I looked it up. It's about four times what most working folks earn.

Why would a retired admiral be living in this dump? Still, it's better than I've ever had before."

"Where did you meet him?" Agatha asked.

"At that bowls club," said Mrs. Nelson. "I'd been drifting around the country, picking up a bit of work here and there, staying in rented rooms, and I ended up in Mircester Park one day. I was standing at the gate in the sunshine watching them playing when he spotted me. He asked me to come in, we got to talking and it all went from there.

"That gave all them at the club something to talk about— and it put that Palmer woman's nose right out of joint. She had her eye on him. She'd known him for years, from way before he were first wed, and he'd been giving her some chat. She's the churchy sort, you know? I'll bet she thought she could save him from the demon drink and all that."

"You were aware that he had a drinking problem, then?" Agatha asked.

"Aware?" Mrs. Nelson laughed. "You couldn't bloody well miss it. He knocked back his Smuggler's Breath morning, noon and night. 'Down the hatch!' That's what he'd yell when he were in a drinking mood—and that were most of the time. Once he'd had a couple, he wouldn't even bother with a glass. He'd swig it straight from the bottle, even at the bowling club, where most of the old biddies only have a small sherry or a half-pint of lager shandy."

"The coroner mentioned painkillers," said Agatha. "What was he taking those for?"

"No idea." Mrs. Nelson shrugged. "I spotted a bottle of

pills in the bathroom cabinet the other day. Never noticed them before. He didn't say what he were taking them for, but why would he? He only ever told me what he wanted to. I bet there's plenty a man like him don't tell his wife."

"Why did he want to get married?" Toni was taking notes on a pad.

"He only wanted a wife for one thing—and no, it's not what you're thinking. There were none of that. We had separate bedrooms. We never actually lived as man and wife in that sense. All he wanted were for me to cook for him, wash his clothes and act like a servant."

"Was it like that right from the start?" asked Agatha.

"Of course!" Mrs. Nelson seemed amazed that she should ask such a question. "That were the arrangement. He'd put a roof over my head and take care of me as long as I kept house for him. It sounded like a good deal to me at first, but after a few years it all turned bad. If I hadn't ironed his shirt properly or got his bowling whites as white as he liked, I could expect a slap."

"I don't think anyone could really blame you for wanting rid of him," said Toni.

"Well, they'd be wrong to think that!" Mrs. Nelson startled Toni with the note of anger in her voice. "We rubbed along just fine and I could handle him when he turned rough. I've known far worse. Every week he'd put money on the table for food and bills. I hated him, sure, but I could put up with him. I didn't want him dead."

"So who would have? Did he have any enemies?" Agatha was fairly sure she already knew the answer to her question.

"Plenty," laughed Mrs. Nelson, stubbing out her cigarette. "He were banned from the local shop for wrecking their booze counter when they wouldn't stock his Smuggler's Breath. Most of the neighbours here hated the sight of him. He came to blows with the old bloke upstairs."

"What was the fight about?" Toni asked.

"Harry had been bragging about being an admiral and related to Admiral Lord Horatio Nelson through the Norfolk side of his family. Bloke upstairs said that if Harry was an admiral then he was Winston Churchill, and the two of them went at it. Pathetic, really. Two old geezers wrestling on the grass outside."

"Which of the other neighbours did he quarrel with?" asked Agatha.

"There was a whole bunch of them in the residents' association." Mrs. Nelson lit another cigarette. "He wanted them all to have canvas screens on their balconies, like they do around the rails on a ship, but no one liked the idea. He could be real charming when he wanted something. He was nice as ninepence at the first of the residents' meetings, but when they wouldn't do what he wanted, he turned nasty and the meetings ended in shouting matches. He didn't have any friends around here."

"He seems to have had a lot of friends at Mircester Crown Green Bowling Club," Toni commented.

"Some of them loved him." Mrs. Nelson smirked, taking a long drag on her cigarette. "They were the ones that fell for his chatty charm and his lies. Then there were the ones that despised him and wanted him kicked out of the club."

"Was Stanley Partridge one of those?" Agatha enquired.

"The little bloke with the glasses?" Mrs. Nelson paused for a second, then nodded. "He seems harmless, but Harry could get him all riled up. Something about wanting to dig up old Stan's rose garden. Funny the things that can wind people up, ain't it?"

"The people who first found him on the bowling green—the Swinburns—they didn't seem to be his biggest fans either," added Agatha.

"Sweet old couple," said Mrs. Nelson. "They came to see me here, asked if there was anything they could do for me. They're nice, but he hated them. She were president, you see? Harry didn't like that. Didn't think a woman should do the job. But he'd already been president and got his little badge. Rules say you can only do it once."

"Will you manage here on your own?" asked Toni.

"I'll be just fine." Mrs. Nelson blew a stream of smoke towards the open balcony doors. "This place is bought and paid for. His pensions ain't much like an admiral's, but they'll come to me now, so I'll be sorted. He'd even set aside money for a fancy funeral—wanted a big party at the bowls club and a flashy headstone in the cemetery. Well, he ain't getting that. Funeral's on Wednesday at the crematorium."

"That's remarkably quick." Agatha knew how far in advance these things had to be booked, and given that the coroner would only have released the body after the inquest on Friday, Wednesday was surprisingly swift.

"They had a cancellation," Mrs. Nelson explained.

"Who cancels a cremation?" Toni looked up from her

pad. "I mean, surely whoever cancelled still has a deceased friend or relative to lay to rest?"

"They do," Mrs. Nelson agreed. "They got in touch with me because they'd been pestering the people that run the cemetery. They asked if I was going to use the plot Harry bought years ago. They were desperate to have a grave to visit. I'm not, so I sold it to them. Those plots are worth a fair bit, you know? Part of the deal was that I got their slot at the crematorium."

"So following Mr. Nelson's death, you now have a home and no real money worries," said Agatha.

"Yeah, but that don't mean I killed him!" Mrs. Nelson stubbed out her cigarette with a series of violent jabs. "That's why I agreed to talk to you. You think he were murdered? Well, I suppose I'm what you'd call your prime suspect, but I didn't do it, see? I was here when he died. Didn't leave the flat all morning."

"Can anyone verify that?" Toni asked. "Was anyone here with you?"

"You mean have I got a proper alibi?" Mrs. Nelson snorted. "Course not. I don't need one. According to the coroner, Harry's death were an accident. But you go shouting your mouth off about murder, Mrs. Raisin, and I'm the one they'll point the finger at. If you get people thinking I killed him, I'll lose the pensions. I'll lose everything and end up in jail—but I didn't do it!"

"If you're innocent, Mrs. Nelson," Agatha assured her, "then you have nothing to worry about."

"Well, I am worried!" A tear appeared on Mrs. Nelson's

cheek. Not a widow's tear shed over the loss of her husband, Agatha noted, but a frightened woman's tear shed over the thought of a stable, secure future being snatched away. "I didn't kill him, I swear!"

"Then the best thing we can do," Agatha said, standing ready to leave, "is to work out who did. Rest assured, Mrs. Nelson, we will find your husband's murderer."

Chapter Seven

"She was hiding something," Agatha said as she and Toni walked back to her car. "Don't get me wrong—she is seriously worried about being accused of murder and she didn't appear to be lying, but there's something she's not telling us. She has something to hide."

"Do you think it's to do with her getting the money from the Admiral's pensions and inheriting that flat?" Toni asked. "She made out that she wouldn't have wanted him dead, yet by her own admission, she's ended up with everything."

"I doubt she realised that would be the way things would work out." Agatha was trying to put herself in Cathy Nelson's position. It wasn't difficult. She had been there. She'd been all alone when she first moved to London, and she'd drifted into a marriage with Jimmy Raisin that had turned very nasty. The difference was, she was smart enough, determined enough and ambitious enough to make something of her life. Cathy Nelson did not have those advantages. "Before he died, I bet she had no idea she would get anything. I think she believed she needed him to provide for her."

"I guess that fits with the reason she gave for marrying him," Toni agreed. "So what do you think she's hiding?"

"I don't know, but she's got a secret, that's for certain." Agatha pressed the button on her key fob to unlock the car. "She covered up some documents so that we wouldn't see them."

"That's a bit careless." Toni frowned, fastening her seat belt. "She saw us arriving. She had plenty of time to hide anything she didn't want us to see. I'd have tucked those papers out of sight if I'd been her."

"But you're not her." Agatha gave a little shake of her head, annoyed at having pointed out something so glaringly obvious. "I mean, she's not as clever as you. She doesn't think like you, so she made a mistake. That's how we catch murderers. We track them down and wait for them to make a mistake."

"So you're counting her as a suspect?"

"Absolutely. She was right about that. She's our prime suspect. She may not have inherited a fortune from the old man, but it sounds like she'll have enough to get by, so she stood to gain from his death and she's not telling us the whole truth. Now, where can I drop you off? I want to head home and change before my meeting at Barfield House."

"I can come with you if you like."

"Thank you, Toni, but this is one I need to handle on my own. Tomorrow, however, is different. The meeting with

Miss Palmer is to do with the Admiral. I know it's a Sunday, but are you free tomorrow morning?"

"Sure," said Toni. "I've nothing else planned."

"Really?" Agatha was surprised. "No new young man you want to spend time with?"

"No." Toni sighed and dropped her head slightly, using her long hair as a screen to avoid eye contact. "I'm footloose and fancy free at the moment."

"Cheer up!" Agatha laughed, starting the engine. "That's the best way to be—ready to take advantage of any opportunity that might come your way. You don't know how lucky you are."

The winding side road that snaked its way into the heart of the countryside off the main road between Mircester and Carsely led, after a few twists and turns, to the gates of Barfield House. Agatha slowed her car to a halt before driving through. There was something different about the old gateway. The stone gateposts, once leaning painfully under their own weight, like pensioners queuing at a bus stop, now stood as straight and tall as guardsmen on parade. The open cast-iron gates, which used to hang like rusty limp flags threatening to collapse into the ground and turn to dust, now displayed themselves like proud banners in shining black and gold. Clearly, things had changed since her previous visit.

Driving through the gateway, Agatha plunged into the shade of the ancient oak and beech trees that lined the drive leading up to the house. Beyond the avenue of trees was an open area of neatly manicured lawn that had, until recently, been so neglected that it had tended to resemble a meadow. The many windows of the reception rooms at the front of the rambling Victorian monstrosity that was Barfield House looked south over the terrace and the largest expanse of lawn, while the imposing main entrance, with its heavy black-studded oak door, was to the side.

Standing on the steps outside the entrance was Gustav, Charles's loyal manservant. He had always openly disapproved of Agatha when she and Charles were close. Having proved her loyalty to Charles in extreme circumstances so many times over the years, she now believed that she had an understanding with Gustav. It was not a friendship. He would never be her friend. One look from his black eyes told her that, and he spoke to her not as a servant might, not even as an equal, but as someone whose presence he merely tolerated. He had that well-practised unwelcoming look on his face as she stepped out of the car. Gustav's every expression was calculated and deliberate. He had the features of a character actor and the wiry physique of a dancer, now held in rigid denial of any form of welcome.

"Good afternoon, Gustav," Agatha called, giving him a huge smile and a cheerful wave to make sure he knew that his posturing was having no effect.

"Mrs. Raisin," he grunted. His accent was unplaceable, certainly giving no hint whatsoever of his Hungarian ancestry. "I saw you arrive."

"That's the second time today someone's seen me

138

coming." Agatha's smile was unwavering. "You'd think a private investigator would be a bit harder to spot, wouldn't you? What's that under your arm?"

"It's a hard hat, Mrs. Raisin," said Gustav, taking the hat in his left hand. "We have various building renovations under way and I must check on their progress shortly."

"So Charles is splashing out and tarting up the old place." Agatha looked up at the scaffolding on the roof. "He must be crashing his way through the pile of cash that came to him after that tragic marriage."

"Not all of us view the death of Sir Charles's wife as a tragedy."

"I meant that it was a tragedy he ever married her in the first place."

"Quite. And to avoid the mayhem that has accompanied some of your previous visits to Barfield House, I decided to intercept you here with a warning. Sir Charles has a surprise in store for you that may not be to your liking. I would rather not have to spend hours clearing up broken china teacups or smashed crystal champagne flutes. We're running a little low on both."

"Thanks for the heads-up, Gustav," Agatha said, climbing the steps to the entrance. "I'll try not to wreck everything." She stopped, turned to face him and nodded her head towards the closed door. He sighed, stepped up to the door, turned the large black iron ring to open it, then marched in ahead of her towards the library, announcing her arrival. She brushed past him to receive an effusive greeting from Charles.

"Aggie, I'm so pleased you could come!" He stepped towards her with his arms out ready to embrace her. She took a step back and shot him a warning look. He lowered his arms.

"Don't call me—" she began.

"Yes, of course." Charles smiled. He was looking fit and slightly tanned, and was as immaculately dressed as ever in a cream shirt and blue chinos. Agatha was glad she had changed into a blue trouser suit to emphasise that she wanted to keep the meeting strictly business. "Let me introduce you to an old friend. Rupert Ferrington-Slade, this is Mrs. Agatha Raisin."

"Delighted to meet you." Ferrington-Slade was younger than Charles and very casually dressed in a polo shirt and jeans. He was also taller than Charles and had rather too much forehead and rather too little chin, which combined to make him look like he was permanently nodding. "Charles has told me so much about . . ."

He froze and his mouth opened wide, mainly to the side as there was so little chin to drop. His eyes narrowed, his nose wrinkled and he retracted the hand he had extended towards Agatha. There then followed an explosive sneeze, most of which he caught in a tissue plucked from a box on a side table.

"Do excuse," he snuffled. "Infernal summer cold. Quite ghastly." Flopping into an armchair, he crumpled the tissue and dropped it in the direction of a waste bin at the side. It missed and joined a cluster of others on the floor.

The two men launched into a conversation about summer

140

colds, hay fever, winter colds and flu. As they talked, Gustav entered with tea and shortbread. Catching a snatch of their conversation, he raised his eyes heavenwards and quickly departed. Agatha sipped her tea and let them talk themselves out, fully aware that both were trying to skirt round the reason for the meeting.

"So what is it you wanted to talk to me about?" she asked when they paused for breath. "I have to tell you that I am not an expert on sniffles and snot."

"Well, yes, um . . . perhaps you could explain, Rupert," said Charles.

"Of course." Rupert snorted to clear his nose. "There's this young filly . . . er . . . young woman lives over in Herris Cum Magna who's just had a sprog . . . a baby . . . and claims the damned thing's mine. I mean, I hardly know the girl. Only met her a few times."

"Where did you meet her?" Agatha asked.

"At a couple of house parties." Ferrington-Slade froze again, then blasted out another sneeze. "First met her at Binky's place." He blew his nose like a hunting horn and dropped another tissue very nearly in the waste bin. "You know Binky, don't you, Charles? He was in the year below you at school. Anyway, what we need you to do, Mrs. Raisin, is find who the real father is and get me off the hook, because this girl is asking for a lot of money to raise the sprog."

"Why don't you insist on a DNA test to prove you're not the father?" asked Agatha.

"Can't be doing with those things." Ferrington-Slade

shook his head vigorously, then passed a soothing hand across his forehead. "I've known chaps stitched up with doctored results, and once they have you on record, you never know who might get hold of your DNA."

"We use a thoroughly reputable and reliable DNA testing service," Agatha explained, "but if you would rather not go down that route for now, I can make some preliminary enquiries."

"Jolly good," said Ferrington-Slade. "Charles, old boy, I think it might be a good idea if I had a little nap before dinner. Would you ask your man to run me a bath? Might clear my passages, you know. Charles will give you the details about the girl in Herris, Mrs. Raisin. I'll take myself off upstairs."

He bade Agatha farewell, and the last she and Charles heard from him was a screeching sneeze from somewhere on the grand staircase.

"He doesn't seem to rate very highly as a philanderer," Agatha commented.

"You mean he's not a devastatingly handsome heartthrob," said Charles. "You'd be amazed how attractive a chap becomes when his family owns so much land and property that he can't actually remember where all their country houses are. He also has a doctorate in history. How would you rate him now?"

"On Snow White's dwarf scale, I'd give him a five out of seven," said Agatha. "He's Grumpy, Dopey, Sleepy, Doc and Sneezy. What he most certainly is not is the reason you wanted me here today."

"There's no fooling you, is there?" Charles nodded. He crossed the room to his desk and tinkled the brass handbell that always sat just to the right of his fountain pen. "Gustav!"

"You howled, Sir Charles?" Gustav appeared an instant later.

"Would you ask our other guests to join us as soon as they're ready, please?"

"Should I run the bath for Snottington-Slime first?"

"Just do it, Gustav." Charles waved him out of the room.

"So your other guests are the real reason you—"

"Hello, Agatha." The woman's voice that came from the doorway had a charming and unmistakable French lilt. Agatha recognised it straight away.

"Claudette," she said, turning to face the newcomer, a grim look on her face. "My, my, this is a surprise."

"*Et moi aussi.*" Pascal Duvivier, Claudette's uncle, caught up with her as she entered the room. "*Bonjour*, Agatha."

Agatha had not seen either of them since an abortive trip to their vineyard in Bordeaux, when she had mistakenly concluded that these people, whom she had come to think of as close friends, had colluded with Charles to arrange the murder of his wife. She also believed they had used her to expose the actual perpetrators of the murder. That she might have been wrong was something that had rankled ever since, although the fact that they had kept important information about the murderers from her had been infuriating. The idea that Charles had also been involved with Claudette without either of them telling her had infuriated her even more.

143

"I . . . I hope you are well." Claudette sounded nervous, apprehensive. "I hope you do not feel—"

"I feel like I've been ambushed, that's how I feel!" Agatha turned to Charles with fire in her eyes. "How could you do this? You lured me here and then sprang a trap? What the hell were you thinking?"

"Please, Agatha, give us a chance to explain," Charles pleaded with her. "You got it all a bit wrong."

"The only thing I got wrong was agreeing to come here!" Agatha snapped. She turned her back on Charles and marched past Claudette and Pascal, putting a huge effort into slamming the heavy library door on her way out. Striding across the enormous expanse of polished wood flooring in the hall, heading for the front door, she skidded to a halt. The slim figure of Mrs. Tassy loomed out of a shadowy corner, her cloud of white hair, pale features and high-necked long dark dress giving her the appearance of a spectre that had stepped out of one of the many ancient paintings scattered around the house.

"Impetuous as always, I see," said the old lady, a stern look in her eyes. "Don't you think you're being a little hasty?"

"I don't like being played," Agatha snarled, "and I don't like their game."

"And you don't like being wrong," added Mrs. Tassy. "I know you may have thought that Charles and those French people had something to do with the death of that dreadful woman he married, but you are most definitely wrong. We can trace our family back more than six centuries,

Mrs. Raisin, and in that time there has been an entire litany of rascals, rogues, scoundrels, reprobates and, yes, even murderers. Charles is not one of them, and you know it. This whole sorry business has been weighing heavy on his mind. His solution—this painful reunion—may be ill-judged and clumsy, but if you care for him, if you ever really cared for him, then go back in there and give him a chance to put things right."

"It's not just Charles," Agatha sighed. "I know he would have gone through hell with his wife and her family and never have considered killing her. It's the Duviviers and the way Charles and Claudette—"

"That's not what you think either." Gustav approached from the direction of his butler's pantry. "You are many things, Mrs. Raisin, but you are not stupid. Blinded by jealousy, perhaps—unfounded jealousy in this case. Mademoiselle Duvivier is not remotely interested in Sir Charles. She prefers younger men and . . . likes to keep her options open, shall we say?"

"No, we shall not." Agatha frowned, beginning to feel that she had walked into another ambush. "What do you mean?"

"He means she rather preferred your company to that of Charles," said Mrs. Tassy.

"Oh . . ." Agatha was taken aback. She was suddenly overwhelmed by a landslide of thoughts and emotions, flattered by Claudette's attention and ashamed that she had spurned her friendship. "But Claudette . . . I mean, I don't . . . I'm not . . ."

145

"She understands that," said Gustav, "but she had come to treasure you as a friend."

"How do you two know all this?" asked Agatha.

"Dear Gustav," said Mrs. Tassy, "has spent years turning listening at keyholes into an art form. I, on the other hand, am very much aware of everything that goes on in this house and have a finely tuned woman's intuition that is one of the few advantages of having lived to such a great age. The question now is: do you have the fortitude to turn around, go back in there and resolve this business?"

Agatha gave Mrs. Tassy a defiant sideways glance, acknowledging the challenge that had been laid down, letting the old lady know that she would not be manipulated, but showing a steely determination. Agatha Raisin did not back down. Agatha Raisin did not give up. Agatha Raisin never ran away from a fight. She walked calmly back to the library and flung open the door.

"Right," she said, standing framed in the doorway. "Let's talk."

The last thing she heard from the hall was a weedy voice on the grand staircase calling, "I say, Gustav old chap . . . what about my bath?"

The clouds that had rolled in over the Cotswolds that day brought no more than a few spots of rain, with the promise of more to come, but put an end to the recent long evenings under clear skies. With the cloud cover came an early dusk, which deepened the hedgerow shadows cast across the deserted country lane. Here and there at the base of the hedges grew tangles of yellow flowers, the common rock rose betraying the way that determined rays of summer sunshine had managed to penetrate the high barriers of hedge foliage. In the trees, blackbirds and starlings competed loudly to sing farewell to the day, almost drowning out the footsteps of an approaching walker.

Dressed in a yellow rain jacket that rivalled the hue of the rock rose, a woman strode confidently down the lane. She paused for a moment and listened carefully. Above the birdsong she could faintly hear a car engine, the vehicle apparently approaching from further up the hill but still out of sight round a bend. She waited with her back to the hedge, giving the car plenty of room to pass by when it got to her, and switching on the torch she carried to make certain she could be seen. She tapped her foot impatiently, the car seeming to take forever to round the bend. When it did finally roll into view, it was travelling only at walking pace. Then, little more than ten yards away, it stopped.

The woman tutted and frowned at the car, unable to make out the driver in the gathering gloom of the evening. Then its headlights illuminated on full beam, forcing her to squint and cover her eyes. The engine revved loudly and the car shot forward, straight towards her. She froze completely for an instant, then turned to run, but managed no more than three paces before the fiercely accelerating vehicle slammed into her. There was a sickening crack as the bumper hit her legs, throwing her feet into the air. Her head hit the bonnet and she cartwheeled crazily backwards, her hip smashing into the windscreen. Such was the force of the impact that she was flung over the roof, crashing down onto the tall hedge and dropping like a discarded rag doll into the field beyond as the car raced off down the lane. Once the sound of its engine had faded into the distance, a blanket of hush fell, even the starlings and blackbirds shocked into silence.

"So you've made up with Charles again?" James was driving Agatha home to Carsely following a thoroughly enjoyable meal at Marco's in Evesham, where they had shared a delicious dish of onglet steak with red-wine shallots and triple-cooked chips. Having tucked into a generous helping of smoked trout and wild garlic pâté to start with, and washed it all down with some excellent wine, Agatha was feeling more sleepy than chatty, especially if the chat was likely to be an awkward one.

"Not in any sense other than that we are now on friendly terms rather than a war footing," she said. "Let's leave it there, James. I'd much rather hear more about that road trip through France you were talking about at dinner."

"Ah, France and *les Français*." James enjoyed rolling his mouth around the pronunciation. "You mentioned they were there this afternoon. How did you leave it with them?"

"They are actually very nice people." Agatha resigned herself to having to explain a little more about that afternoon's ambush. "I got it wrong about them being involved with the murder. It seemed to be obvious at the time, especially as there was information they had chosen not to share with me, but I don't now believe they had anything to do with Charles's wife's death, and . . . Look! What's going on there?"

They were just about to turn off the A44 onto the road that would take them down into Carsely. In the field to their right was the blazing wreck of a car, flames leaping twenty feet in the air, lighting up the night.

"We should stop," Agatha suggested, transfixed.

"There's no need," said James, flicking the turn signal to leave the main road. "Look at all those flashing blue lights. The fire brigade are there, and the police. This one's nothing to do with you, my dear. Just joyriders, I expect."

"Yes," she agreed. "I suppose you're right. No need to get involved, and I have a fairly early start tomorrow morning anyway. Home, please, James. I'm knackered."

The road out of Carsely, heading to the A44 at the top of the village, was almost a tunnel of trees, their branches reaching out to embrace those growing from the opposite side like fondly remembered friends separated by the long, cold, leafless months of winter. All that seemed to stop the summer foliage from swooping down to block the road completely was the regular bus service to Mircester. You could judge the height of the double-decker bus by the arch that the branches formed to allow it to pass underneath. Any fresh young limbs daring to dive down into the tunnel were savagely whisked away by its roof. The roof of

149

Toni's small car, in which she was driving Agatha to their Sunday-morning meeting, posed no such danger to the overhanging branches.

Willow Way was a long, narrow road dipping down to the right towards a river where a cluster of willow trees dangled their branches over the water like creatures from a forgotten time gathered to drink together. The river was not as wide at this point as it was when it reached Carsely, but it still ran powerfully deep, with brown trout sheltering in the shade of its banks and bullheads hiding under its stones. There was neither pavement nor grass verge at the sides of the road, and when they encountered a van coming in the opposite direction, Toni slowed to a crawl, the two vehicles inching past each other, the leaves and twigs of the tall roadside hedgerows rustling and squeaking against their paintwork. She and the driver exchanged a cheery wave.

Rounding the next bend, they came to Willow Cottages. The small terrace of farm cottages nestled shyly in a gap in the hedgerow, their neatly cut Cotswold stone walls set beneath tiled, rather than thatched, roofs. Each had a parking space, and Toni pulled into the one in front of Miss Palmer's cottage at the end of the row. Agatha eased herself out of the little car, smoothed the sitting creases on her dress and loosened the straps on the red sandals she was trying to break in.

"Looks like a nice place to live," Toni commented.

"A little isolated," said Agatha, mentally comparing the cottages to her own, which was in the heart of Carsely, and deciding they didn't quite come up to scratch, "and a bit on the small side, but quite pleasant."

The front door was painted black, as were all the others in the terrace, and boasted a splendid brass lion's-paw knocker. Agatha rapped the knocker and they waited. There was no sound of any sort from inside the cottage. She knocked again. Still nothing.

"That's strange," she said, checking her watch. "She should be home from church by now."

"Excuse me." A woman's voice came from the front door of the adjacent cottage. A middle-aged couple were standing on the doorstep. "Are you looking for Miss Palmer?"

"Yes," Agatha said. "She asked us to meet her here after church."

"We didn't see her set off for church this morning," said the woman. "She walks, you know. She's a great one for her walking. She walks for an hour down beyond the willows at the bridge every evening, and walks into Carsely most days."

"We didn't see her on the way here," said Toni.

"No," Agatha agreed. She made a quick phone call to Mrs. Bloxby, who confirmed that Miss Palmer hadn't been at church that morning.

"This is weird." Agatha frowned, then turned to the neighbours. "It's all a bit worrying. You clearly know Miss Palmer quite well. Do you have keys to her house? I think we should check inside."

"George," said the woman to her husband. "Fetch the spare keys."

The woman introduced herself as Mrs. Leeds before accompanying Agatha and Toni into Miss Palmer's house, clearly concerned about her neighbour but also unwilling to give two complete strangers unfettered access to the property.

"You'll understand that I can't be leaving you alone in here," she said. "You hear such shocking stories nowadays, don't you? Con merchants and scammers and suchlike."

"Quite right," said Agatha, "but we must check that nothing's happened to Miss Palmer. Why don't you lead the way?"

There was a tidy sitting room off the main entrance hall at the front of the house and a small kitchen leading out onto a garden at the rear. Upstairs were two bedrooms and a bathroom, but no sign at all of Miss Palmer. They made their way back down to the sitting room, where a small desk nestled snugly beneath the front window. Agatha stroked a hand gently across the keys of the typewriter sitting on the desk.

"My goodness," she said. "A Remington Monarch. I haven't seen one of these for years."

"I didn't know you were an expert on typewriters," said Toni.

"I trained as a shorthand typist before I went into PR," Agatha explained. "I think this confirms where our typed note came from."

"So Miss Palmer normally walked in that direction every evening, Mrs. Leeds?" Toni asked, looking out of the front window down the lane as far as the hedgerows would allow.

"She did," said Mrs. Leeds. "Sometimes quite late. Liked a walk before bed to help her sleep sound. Always took a torch when the light was failing. You don't think anything's happened to her, do you?"

"I'm sure everything's fine," Agatha reassured her. "She must have been delayed somewhere. We'll take a look around outside. Come on, Toni."

They walked out past Toni's car and turned right to head downhill towards the river. There was a slight bend in the road before a long straight stretch opened out ahead of them.

"What are those?" Toni pointed into the sky, where a handful of large birds were circling. "They're huge. They look like vultures."

"Not quite," said Agatha, recognising the birds' splayed wingtip feathers and distinctive forked tails. "They're red kites, but they're prone to scavenging like vultures. Look at the hedge here. The top is even and level up to this point, then lower and broken, as though it's had something heavy land on it. We need to take a look in the field on the other side."

"There's a small gap in the hedge just there." Toni walked towards a split in the hedge and hauled aside a branch or two. "I think we could make it through."

With a little effort, and some language more at home in a barrack room than on a country ramble, they forced their way through the hedge into a field of bare earth, its crop of rapeseed having recently been harvested. Toni was picking twigs and bugs out of her hair when Agatha's red sandals landed on the bare earth in front of her.

153

"Snakes and bastards!" Having flung off her shoes, Agatha was running as fast as she could across the ploughed field. Ahead of her lay the body of a woman dressed in a tweed skirt, yellow rain jacket and walking shoes.

Agatha was bent over the body when Toni caught up.

"It's Miss Palmer," Agatha said, staring at the congealed blood matted in the woman's grey hair. "She's dead. Stone cold. She must have been here all night."

For a moment they both fell silent, looking down at the broken body on the ground.

"Awful," Agatha said faintly. "Always the same. It looks like a person but there's really nothing of that person left. She's gone. So not a person—a body."

"Look at the tracks in the soil," Toni said, indicating drag marks in the soft earth. "It looks like she crawled here."

"Those tracks lead back to the hedge, where the top's damaged," Agatha said, sitting back on her heels and studying the scene, allowing her imagination to run through the probable events of the night before. "I'd say she crawled here to get away from the road, or maybe because she was confused. The dent in the top of the hedge could be from where a body landed on it—a body flung into the air when it was hit by a vehicle out on the road."

"The poor woman," said Toni. "She must have been in dreadful pain, and she died out here in a cold field, all alone."

"And before she had the chance to talk to us."

"You mean someone did this deliberately to stop her from talking? You think she was murdered?"

"That's exactly what I think. She walked on that road every night. It's narrow, but it's quiet, and she must have known it well. She would have known how to stay safe. She would have been able to hear a car coming and give it plenty of room. Look, there's her torch—still in her hand."

"It's switched on," Toni said, examining it without touching it, "but there's no light. The battery must have died."

"We need to call this in," Agatha sighed, reaching for her phone.

Having reported their discovery, they were told to stay exactly where they were and wait for the police to arrive. Agatha had just ended the call when a large, heavy raindrop splotted on her phone's screen. She and Toni shared a look of pained resignation. Soon the rain was battering down like a tropical deluge. They slipped and slithered across the mud, the field having turned into an instant quagmire, and stopped where Agatha had abandoned her sandals. Toni squeezed through the sodden hedge while Agatha put on her shoes. Agatha chose to try minimising the vicious scratches the hedge could inflict by backing through it. She got halfway, then became so snagged on twigs and branches that she could barely move.

"Toni!" she yelled above the rain slashing through the foliage and beating down on the road. "A little help here, please?"

Toni, her hair soaked flat on her head and clinging to her face, reached out to grab Agatha's hips and pulled. They both stumbled into the road, drenched and muddied, make-up smearing their faces and bits of hedge entwined in their clothes.

"You know that phrase about looking like you've been dragged through a hedge backwards?" Agatha asked.

Toni nodded. Agatha pointed to herself.

"What about looking like a drowned rat?" Toni asked.

Agatha nodded. Toni pointed to herself.

A moment later, a police car arrived, bringing two officers Agatha vaguely recognised. The first moved quickly to check the body while the other blocked the road with cones and blue and white tape. The next car arrived hot on its heels, and Agatha was relieved to see Bill Wong step out, accompanied by a young constable she didn't know.

"Agatha!" he called, rushing over to her. "Are you okay?"

"I'm fine," Agatha assured him. "I can't say the same for poor Miss Palmer, though."

She explained how they had found the body, and Bill went to talk to the officer who had gone into the field. Agatha glanced at Toni, whose thin cotton top was wet through.

"Toni!" she hissed, nodding at the younger woman's chest. "A bra might have been a good idea. This is a murder investigation, not a wet T-shirt contest!"

Toni looked down at herself, appalled, and folded her arms. The young constable handed Agatha a blanket and draped a bright green high-vis police rain jacket over Toni's shoulders. Bill returned to talk to Agatha, peering out from beneath the hood of his own waterproof jacket and steering her to a relatively sheltered spot close to Miss Palmer's cottage.

"I have to get things organised here," he said, struggling to make himself heard above the torrential rain. "Toni will have to leave her car for the time being. If you can both go to your house, I will join you there later. Paul will drive you." He nodded towards the young constable, now chatting to Toni beneath the shelter of a nearby tree.

"So, Paul," said Agatha, sitting alongside Toni in the back seat of the police car. "Would it be 'Paul Easeman,' by any chance?"

"Ah." The young officer glanced back from the driver's seat, giving her a sheepish grin. "Paul Hastings, actually. Um . . . sorry about the prank the other day."

Agatha's bear-like eyes stared coldly from behind a smeared palette of smudged mascara and rain-streaked make-up.

"Just drive, PC Hastings."

Chapter Eight

Agatha stared quizzically at Roy, pouring him a coffee and sitting down to help herself to the toasted bagels with smoked salmon and cream cheese that he had prepared.

"Roy," she asked eventually, "what exactly are you wearing?"

Roy plucked at one of the multitude of pockets in the one-piece orange overalls he had appeared in that morning.

"Working overalls, darling," he said. "There are showers forecast all day, so there will be no play at the club, but I've been drafted onto the renovation committee. We're tarting up the little kitchen and repainting the main room in the clubhouse."

"That sounds a bit like manual labour to me," said Agatha. "I wouldn't have thought it was your thing."

"I can do my bit when it's needed," Roy defended himself with a voice deliberately overloaded with insulted drama. "These bagels are fabulous, aren't they? Got them from a little baker in Mircester yesterday. Who'd have thought you could get bagels this good outside of London?"

"They're fantastic," Agatha agreed, taking another mouthful. "You're spoiling me."

"Well, you didn't have a proper dinner last night, did you? Bill Wong was here for an absolute age questioning you about the body in the field."

"He needs as much ammunition as he can get in order to link this to the death of the Admiral. Wilkes is adamant they are unrelated. The Admiral was an accident and this was a hit-and-run by joyriders who then torched the car they'd stolen."

"He's such an idiot. Anyway, I'm hoping to pick up a bit more gossip today—people love to chat while they're working. I couldn't update you last night, but I can tell you now that the bowling club is a hotbed of intrigue."

"I know the Admiral was someone the members either loved or hated."

"Not just him, but the current president too. Mrs. Swinburn has made the club more family friendly. She's allowed children into the clubhouse to make it easier for parents or grandparents to use the place, but there are plenty who see it as somewhere to get away from their kids. They were right behind the Admiral when he was president and banned kids from the club. Seems he hated children even more than he hated Mrs. Swinburn and her husband. He was against absolutely everything they tried to do to improve the place. That's a dreadful shame really, because they devote all their time to it and they're such awfully nice people."

"Morning, Mrs. Raisin!" Doris Simpson's voice echoed through from the hall. She had let herself in as usual with keys provided by Agatha. Monday was her cleaning day. "Oh, and Mr. Silver, too," she added, poking her head round the kitchen door. "Shall I start upstairs? I saw the bin men were on their way. I'll tidy up outside once they're gone if you like. They're a messy lot, that crew. Lots of my regulars have been complaining about them leaving a trail of rubbish and tampering with the bins. I mean, why on earth would anyone tamper with a bin?"

"Why indeed?" Agatha mused, taking a final sip of coffee. "Roy, if you see James, will you tell him that I'm meeting Claudette for lunch at The Feathers in Ancombe? He's welcome to join us if he's around. I'd love him to meet her."

She grabbed her handbag and was making her way down the front path to her car when she heard a cheery "Mornin', missus!" Outside her front gate, Simon was leaning on her wheelie bin, wearing a bin man's work clothes and a cheeky grin. As she drew nearer, he lowered his head and his voice.

"I'm on to something with this crew," he mumbled. "They're different from the others. They're up to no good all right."

"Cut the chat! We don't have all day!" The refuse truck driver was leaning out of the cab window. His shaven head had a crop of dark stubble that matched the shadow on his fleshy face. Agatha felt there was something vaguely familiar about him, but dismissed the notion given that his general appearance was so similar to that of many other workmen and labourers. Then he spoke again. "Get a move on, you useless pillocks!"

That was it! It was his voice that was familiar, not his face! She had never seen his face. He was the man who had been organising the Romanian animal smugglers in the woods behind Eric Collins's house. He must be the one who'd got away in the Land Rover when Blackbeard and his gang were arrested. She found herself staring at him, and suddenly realised that he was staring straight back at her. From the look in his cold grey eyes, she had no doubt that he knew exactly who she was. He must have been watching when she had stalled Blackbeard by the gates at the farm compound.

"See you later, boss," Simon said quietly and headed off to climb back aboard the truck, which then rumbled noisily out of Lilac Lane.

"Bill," Agatha's phone was in her hand before the truck was even out of sight, "the one that got away in the green Land Rover at the farm is currently driving round Carsely in a bin lorry with Simon on board . . ."

As soon as Agatha reached the office, she briefed Patrick on the situation with the refuse truck. He in turn informed their client that one of his crews had a wanted man in charge and that the police were after them. She then settled behind her desk with that morning's *Mircester Telegraph* to read about the body found in the field off Willow Way. DCI Wilkes was quoted at length, clearly delighted to be getting his name and photograph in the paper. Toni ventured into Agatha's office when she saw her reading the report.

"Have you seen what Wilkes is saying?" Agatha held up the newspaper. "He told Charlotte Clark that Miss Palmer's death was 'a tragic accident involving a vehicle stolen that afternoon in Mircester and later set alight,' and he's appealing for witnesses."

"So I read," said Toni. "We didn't get a mention at all."

"I asked Charlotte to keep us out of it for the time being," Agatha admitted. "I don't want the murderer to know that we're linking this to the death of the Admiral."

"Surely he—or she—would be silly not to realise that?" said Toni. "We're not exactly amateurs."

"No, but our murderer is. Poisoning with weedkiller isn't an effective way to kill someone—even an eighty-five-year-old. What if the Admiral had survived? What if he'd lived long enough to whisper in my ear who'd done it?"

"I suppose Miss Palmer's murder is the same. Hitting her with a car couldn't guarantee she would die straight away, and in fact, she didn't. The poor thing was able to drag herself away from the hedge. What if she'd still been alive when we got to her? Maybe she'd have told us who was driving the car."

"Exactly. See if you can dig up a bit more background on Miss Palmer, Toni, and her neighbours in Willow Way. We need to know more about her."

Agatha spent most of the morning on client reports and on the Deirdre Higginbotham notes, but the murders of the Admiral and Miss Palmer were never far from her mind. After a while, she cast everything else aside and went through Toni's notes from the meeting with Cathy Nelson. There was something very wrong about the woman, she decided, and she was determined to find out what it was. Before she left for lunch, she asked Toni and Patrick to go door-to-door at the Admiral's apartment block to see what they could find out about Mrs. Nelson and to dig up whatever they could on the neighbours, especially the one the Admiral had brawled with.

With the weather beginning to brighten and only an occasional shower sweeping across the countryside, Agatha enjoyed the short drive to Ancombe. Mircester wasn't really such a bad place, and the older part of the town was really quite pretty, but Ancombe was something special. The village was only two miles from Carsely and it was a little-known Cotswolds gem, with its cluster of thatched cottages each competing to surround itself with the best kept garden, its ancient church and its pub, The Feathers. Lunch at The Feathers, renowned for its slightly pretentious but nonetheless delicious cuisine, was always a real treat. The fact that she was lunching with Claudette and that both of them seemed determined to put their friendship back on a firm footing made the anticipation all the more intense.

Just as Agatha pulled into the car park at The Feathers, her phone rang. It was Bill Wong.

"We've found the bin lorry abandoned on the council estate outside Carsely," he said, "and there are traces of what we think is probably cocaine, PCP and a range of other Class A drugs in the cab. Sadly, there's no trace of the crew."

"They can't all have simply vanished," said Agatha, "and the cab must be covered in fingerprints. You must know who some of them are."

"We do, Agatha. Most of them are local lads and we'll round them up quite quickly, I'm sure. The driver, however, is a different kettle of fish. We've no idea who he is. I think you're right about him recognising you from the farm compound. He must have realised the game was up, and that's why they all disappeared."

"What about Simon?"

"If he was undercover, my guess is he's hanging out with one or two of the local lads, or maybe he's lying low until he can make his way to your office. He wasn't with you at the farm, so the driver won't have recognised him. I'm sure he's fine. It's you I'm worried about. If Blackbeard's organisation was involved in smuggling and distributing drugs as well as trafficking endangered species—and it looks like they were—and you've brought down both those operations, they'll be out to get you."

"Well, I'm not about to let that put me off my lunch." Agatha said her goodbyes and headed into The Feathers.

"Agatha! I am so happy to see you!" Claudette rose from the table, threw her arms around Agatha and kissed her on both cheeks. "And I adore this place. It is so very English, *non*? My eyes could not believe it when Sir Charles dropped me off. I think he would stay, but I tell him this lunch is just for me and for you."

"Good." Agatha took her seat, careful not to ruck the

tablecloth and tip over the sparkling slim-stemmed wine glasses. "That's exactly as I want it. Have you been able to help Charles with his vineyard plans?"

"A little, maybe. In the Cotswolds there are a few wine houses, you know? Some produce blended wine, some have single-grape varietals; they use Chardonnay and Bacchus and a few others. He really needs to talk to these growers, *non*? They will share their knowledge, unlike in France, where we keep our wine-making secrets to ourselves!" Claudette laughed, her brown eyes sparkling and her long dark hair spilling over her shoulders. "In England they will share, because if one has success, it is good news for the others also."

Once they had ordered, their conversation turned to Ancombe and its famous mineral water spring. That led to Agatha telling Claudette all about how she had become involved with two murders in the village when she had been working as a PR consultant for the Ancombe Water Company. Despite Claudette's morbid delight in hearing about the grisly deaths, Agatha steered the conversation away from murder and onto the Frenchwoman's show-jumping exploits. It wasn't long, of course, before their chat turned to her handsome uncle, Pascal.

"I think he was most fond of you," said Claudette.

"And I him," Agatha agreed. "Your wonderful chateau is such a beautiful place that there was certainly romance in the air when Pascal and I sat chatting into the wee small hours, but it wasn't to be. Too many complications."

Her phone rang before the subject could be unravelled any further, and she gratefully jumped at the chance to answer it.

"Hello . . . Aga . . . news . . . Simo . . ."

"Bill, is that you?" Agatha pressed the phone closer to her ear. "You're breaking up. I'll call you back." She turned to Claudette. "I'm sorry, but this might be important."

"But of course." Claudette smiled. "We are almost finished, yes? Pascal will be here to pick me up any time now."

"I can get better reception outside," said Agatha, heading for the door.

Walking from Carsely to Ancombe had taken James a little longer than he'd expected, but he hadn't pushed the pace. It had been more of a stroll, if he was honest with himself, not the marching pace he'd been used to in the army. He had, however, built up a bit of a thirst and paused at the Ancombe fountain, where the spring water gushed out of the mouth of a stone skull. He stooped to rinse his hands and then cupped them under the flowing water to take a drink. It was then that he saw Agatha emerge from The Feathers. He was about to call out to her when a broad-shouldered, dark-haired man approached her. That, he told himself, must be Pascal, the Frenchie she had talked about. He crouched out of sight by the fountain.

"Pascal." Agatha raised her eyes from her phone when she realised who was standing in front of her. "You surprised me."

"I am collecting Claudette," he said, the soft, deep voice

heavy with his warm, sultry French accent, "but I hoped I would see you."

"I . . . sort of hoped the same," she admitted.

"I have missed you."

"Since Saturday?"

"You joke, but yes, since Saturday and since your visit to the chateau. I have thought about you many times. You spread through my mind. I think about you every day."

"I often think about that first visit to the chateau. There was something very special about it. It was magical. I have missed you too."

"Then you understand. You know that there was something between us in Bordeaux. I felt it. It was so strong, so powerful. I know you felt it also."

"Yes, but I—"

He took her in his arms and they kissed, then she pulled away.

"Oh Pascal," she breathed, an undeniable note of sadness in her voice. "This isn't meant to be. It isn't right for me, and if we were to . . . well, it would be a disaster for both of us." She threw her arms around him and held him close. "Let's not spoil things. We mustn't play with each other's feelings. That would ruin everything. We must stay good friends."

"If that is all there is," he smiled, "then it will be a painful friendship, but a pain I will happily bear. One day, perhaps, the wind will change. It will blow away the clouds in your head and you will see that we should be more than just the good friends."

He kissed her again, then she smiled, said goodbye and headed for the car park and solid phone reception. Pascal made his way into The Feathers. James stood slowly, turned and headed home to Carsely.

As soon as she was clear of the building, Agatha's call went through to Bill.

"Agatha, thank goodness," he said, clearly speaking from a vehicle in motion. "Get down to the hospital in Mircester. Simon's been hurt."

"Hurt?" Agatha demanded. "What does that mean? How bad is he? What's happened to him?"

"No details yet," Bill reported. "I'll see you there."

Agatha dashed to her car and screeched out of the car park, heading for Mircester.

The air in the small clearing was filled with the robust smell of damp earth and softly decaying leaves. A thin mist of evaporating moisture sown with forest dust turned the momentary cloud-break sunshine that filtered through the trees into beams of light. Vivid colours were revealed where the light played at the base of a tree or pooled on the mossy forest floor. In this place where the sway of branches, the whisper of foliage and the orchestra of birdsong were the elemental background music, the static crackle of an electronic device could not have sounded more alien. Neither did the two human voices have any place in this tranquil setting.

"It all has to shut down. She's left us with no option."

"Where did she come from? Why have you let this happen?"

"She blundered in on us when we could never have expected it."

"Mistakes were made. We made it easy for her."

"We need to let things calm down, then we can start up again."

"We must learn from our mistakes, eradicate error."

"She's turned out to be our biggest mistake."

"Then get rid of her."

There was a click as the caller hung up and the hands-free car phone fell silent. The driver slammed the door, the engine coughed into life and the green Land Rover slithered off up the forest track.

Agatha dashed from the hospital car park to the Accident and Emergency entrance and was directed from the reception desk along a corridor. The windowless passage seemed endless and, like all hospital corridors, was lit in a way that was so far removed from daylight that it made you feel as if you were in a submarine or a spaceship. At last she turned a corner and saw Bill Wong talking to a young male doctor.

"How is he?" she gasped, rushing up to Bill.

"Looks like he has a broken nose, a fractured cheekbone and concussion," said Bill. "He's conscious and the doctor says we can go in to talk to him."

The doctor showed them into a curtained cubicle, where Simon lay propped up on a bed. He had a bloody gash across the bridge of his nose, which, like his right cheek, was red, swollen and deformed. Black rings were starting to form under his eyes, and he was hooked up to a bedside monitor. An attractive female nurse was gently cleaning caked blood off his chin, but stopped when she saw Agatha and Bill.

"Don't keep him too long," she said. "He tires easily and we need to move him up to a ward shortly."

"Thank you, Nurse," said Bill.

"Not bad, eh?" Simon croaked weakly once she had gone. "She promised me her number if I behave."

"Simon," Agatha said in a remorseful voice. "I'm so sorry. I should never have sent you . . ."

"Don't go getting all mushy on me, boss." Simon managed a thin smile.

"I do not get 'mushy.'" She bristled.

"That's better," he replied, and Agatha smiled, shaking her head. Even from his hospital bed he was managing to wind her up. "It was my job, boss. Now listen. I get a bit dizzy and woozy . . . bit sleepy . . . concussion. The driver . . . he's the main man."

"What's his name?" asked Bill.

"They call him Carver . . . green Land Rover . . ." said Simon.

"From what we've discovered," said Bill, "it looks like their customers were taping payment envelopes inside the bin lids, and received their deliveries in return the same way."

"Correct . . ." Simon made a little clicking noise in his

170

cheek, moved his hands in an attempt to clap, then let them fall back on the bed. Agatha hated that game-show-host move, but wished with all her heart that he'd been able to do it. He let out a shallow breath and his eyes closed.

"Nurse!" Agatha screeched, and the pretty nurse rushed back in. She felt Simon's pulse, checked the monitor and relaxed.

"He's sleeping," she said with a reassuring smile. "Best thing for him right now. He needs rest. I'll keep an eye on him, don't worry."

Agatha and Bill left the cubicle and made their way towards the exit.

"What happened to him, Bill?" Agatha asked.

"He was found under a hydrangea bush in a garden on the outskirts of Carsely. Clearly he'd been hit pretty hard in the face, and a shovel was found nearby with bloodstains. I think Carver must have seen him talking to you and figured out that he was a plant working for you. He smacked him with the shovel and drove off quick as he could to find a place where they could abandon the truck and scarper."

"I'm going to get this Carver bloke," Agatha swore. "I'll make him wish he'd never clapped eyes on me!"

Agatha returned to her office and phoned Claudette to explain her abrupt departure. The young Frenchwoman's voice was full of concern for Simon. She said she had decided to extend her stay for a few days and hoped they would have the chance to meet again before she returned to Bordeaux. Struggling to concentrate on any work, Agatha turned away from her desk to look out of the window and saw two familiar figures in the street, looking up at her and waving. It was the Swinburns. She waved back, signalled to them to wait, and trotted downstairs.

"Mr. and Mrs. Swinburn." She tiptoed across the cobbles and greeted them with handshakes. "How nice to see you."

"We wanted to talk to you, Mrs. Raisin, but I wasn't sure I could manage the stairs," said Mrs. Swinburn. "It's too important for the telephone."

"Really?" said Agatha. "Why don't we walk down the lane here? This is the nicest part of old Mircester, and there's a lovely tea shop near the abbey."

"We know it," said Mr. Swinburn. "It's our favourite."

"They do a lovely Chelsea bun," added Mrs. Swinburn. "We usually share one between us."

They sat at a round table in the multi-paned bow window of the Abbey Tea Shop, looking out at the towering stone walls of Mircester's medieval abbey, which dominated this part of the town.

"Now, what did you want to talk to me about?" Agatha asked, as a waitress appeared with a laden tea trolley, setting china cups and saucers on the table.

"It's about the Admiral," said Mrs. Swinburn. "Everyone at the bowling club read what you said in the *Telegraph*. You said you thought he was murdered."

"That's true." Agatha took a sip of tea. "I do."

"Well, what with that and what happened to Miss Palmer,"

said Mr. Swinburn, "it's got people at the club talking, and some of them are saying that *we* killed both of them!"

"Surely not," said Agatha. "Why would they think that?"

"Because we've known them both for years," Mrs. Swinburn explained. "Miss Palmer—Dorothy—used to work for us."

"We had a lovely little business." Mr. Swinburn beamed with pride. "Not so little by the time we sold up and retired. Car repairs and servicing. Always an honest job and everyone knew they could rely on us to—"

"Yes, yes, not now, Charlie," his wife interrupted him. 'That's not what we're here to talk about. Let me tell Mrs. Raisin—you'll just get it all wrong.

"We'd all known each other since our schooldays. Miss Palmer always had a soft spot for Harry Nelson, but he was three or four years older and never paid her any attention. When he came home from the sea, he would go crazy, drinking and chasing after girls. He was a good-looking lad too, back in those days. Then he got that girl pregnant—"

"His first wife, Constance?" Agatha interrupted, looking for clarification.

"Yes, Connie, but they weren't married then." Mrs. Swinburn was quite positive. "He got her pregnant, then ran off back to the navy. Well, she was still in her teens, and in those days it was unthinkable for a young girl to be an unmarried mother. There was a real stigma. The family would be disgraced. Before she started to get too big to hide the fact that she was pregnant, her parents sent her off to live with her aunt in Worcester. When the baby was born, it was given

173

away for adoption. Connie came home, and it was never spoken about."

"That seems so cruel." Agatha was aghast.

"That's the way things were done back then, Mrs. Raisin," Mrs. Swinburn insisted, "and Harry Nelson would never have made any kind of a father. He always hated children. That didn't put Connie off him, though. When he was next home, they took up again and they eventually married. Miss Palmer was heartbroken."

"And I believe the marriage ended in tragedy," said Agatha.

"A terrible tragedy. Harry was home on leave when he found out she was pregnant again. Soon after that, she fell out of the window, although there were plenty who didn't believe she just fell. He never wanted children, and some say he made her life such a living hell that she jumped. There were others said he flung her out. Whatever the truth was, he was never prosecuted and went back to the navy. No one saw hide nor hair of him for years after that. We built up our business and Miss Palmer worked with us until we all retired. She never married."

"Was she involved with the bowling club?" Agatha asked.

"She was. Then Harry Nelson turned up in Mircester again and he joined the club too. He used to make a real nuisance of himself, but Miss Palmer was always the one to calm him down when he was having one of his drunken rants. Even after all those years, she still thought she could see something good in him.

"That Cathy woman suddenly appeared about eight years

174

ago, and they were married within months. Miss Palmer couldn't stand the sight of her. She refused to accept that they were wed. She said it was all wrong, and she couldn't stand the sight of them together. She resigned from the club and never set foot in the place again."

"And the Admiral became club president?" Agatha was engrossed in the story.

"He did. Four years ago. The members vote for a new president every three years and you can only be president once. He nearly ruined the club when he was in charge. He banned children, he had the bar open all hours, he wanted a separate area for women . . ."

"I heard he wanted to dig up the rose garden," Agatha added.

"Yes indeed. Stan was furious with him about that. Fortunately, I took over as president before he could do away with the roses." She stroked the gold president's badge on her lapel. "We've spent most of my first year in the post putting right the things that he did. He hated me being president. He didn't think a woman should be in charge of anything, let alone Mircester Crown Green Bowling Club. When Charlie told people that he would run for president in two years when I stand down, Harry went wild. He said we were trying to take over the place and started trying to have the rule overturned so that he could have another go.

"Then he died, and now Miss Palmer's dead, and some people are blaming us!" Mrs. Swinburn was wringing her hands. "They're talking about banning Charlie from being president and even throwing us out of the club." Tears were welling in her eyes and she reached into her handbag for a tissue.

"That's why we wanted to talk to you, Mrs. Raisin." Mr. Swinburn took over. "We want to engage you to investigate this business and find out who killed the Admiral. If that means finding Dorothy Palmer's murderer too, then that's all to the good."

"You know, of course, that I'm already looking into the Admiral's murder," Agatha pointed out.

"But we will pay you, Mrs. Raisin." Mrs. Swinburn was almost pleading. "Please set aside everything else and concentrate on this. We need you to make sure that no one can call our reputations into question—and that means catching the killer!"

The afternoon was growing late when Agatha got back to her office. Toni and Patrick were out on enquiries. Helen offered her a cup of tea, which she refused, then a gin and tonic, which she accepted. She then spent an eternity trying to get through to someone at the hospital who could update her on Simon, eventually reaching the ward sister by claiming she was Simon's mother.

"I need to know how he's doing," she said.

"And you're his mother?" the sister asked.

"Um . . . yes," Agatha lied.

"That's strange, because his mother is sitting by his bedside right now."

"Ah . . . I'm . . . his other mother."

"Simon!" Agatha heard the sister calling. "Your other mother's on the phone."

"Ha! It's the boss!" She heard Simon's unmistakable guffaw in the background, then, "Ow! It hurts when I laugh!"

"As you can probably hear," the sister came back on the line, "he's awake again and in reasonably good spirits. He'll be with us overnight so we can monitor the concussion, and probably a couple of days longer while the damage to his cheek is assessed, although it's not expected that he will need any major reconstruction."

Agatha asked her to pass on her best wishes, and just as she hung up, the ever-efficient Helen appeared in her office with a get-well card for her to sign. She made notes about the conversation with the Swinburns, then decided to head for home.

Driving along the main A44, Agatha was looking forward to seeing James. She wanted to tell him about Simon and how the animal traffickers had also turned out to be drug smugglers. She wanted to tell him about the Swinburns and what she'd learned about the Admiral. She wanted to discuss all of that with him. She decided against telling him about Pascal. That was something best left to drift off into the past. That was something . . . A car came racing up behind her, dodging from side to side in her rear-view mirror. What the hell was the maniac playing at? Why didn't he just overtake if he wanted to? There was plenty of space. The car surged forward, then there was an impact that sounded almost as loud as a cannon blast and Agatha's car slewed sideways. She wrestled with the steering wheel to keep heading in a straight line as the car behind hit her again with another resounding thump and the sound of one of her rear lights smashing.

She pressed her right foot to the floor, accelerating to try outrunning her attacker, but the other car kept pace, hitting her again and again. She saw the turning for Carsely coming up and yanked the wheel over, taking the corner much too fast, her tyres squealing and fighting for grip. It was as if the other driver had predicted her move and the car stayed within inches of Agatha's, almost like it was chained to her bumper. She began to panic. What could she do? The lunatic was trying to kill her. She couldn't drive home and get out. She wouldn't stand a chance of making it into her house and locking the door before whoever it was got hold of her. She risked a glance in the mirror but couldn't see the other driver and quickly concentrated ahead, the roadside trees flashing past faster than she had ever known.

She saw Willow Way coming up to the left. Of course—Miss Palmer's place! It might still be a crime scene. There might be an officer stationed there! She stamped on her brakes to take the turn and the car behind slammed into her, almost pushing her past the entrance to the lane. She accelerated hard, sounding her horn to attract the attention of any officer on duty further down the road. As she hurtled past Miss Palmer's cottage, horn blaring, she screamed with relief when she saw a police car parked there. The car in pursuit, however, was right on her tail, and a moment later, the bridge, fringed by willows, was in sight.

The road here widened slightly, and to her horror, the

other car drew level and side-swiped her, the bodywork of both vehicles crunching and buckling. The second swipe was even more violent, and Agatha's car lurched off the road, bumping and crashing down an embankment onto a sloping stretch of grass, on a collision course with a very solid-looking willow trunk. She yanked the steering wheel to the left, her effort and the slope combining to roll the car onto its side, onto its roof, then onto its other side. There were multiple detonations as the airbags deployed, filling the car with a powdery dust, and Agatha felt her seat belt bite into her shoulder and her hips as the car rolled. The airbags deflated in a heartbeat and she realised the car was still moving, crunching and scraping along on its side, heading straight for the river.

She screamed as it ploughed into the water, sending up a fountain of spray and steam before rolling violently onto its roof again. She had time to see water fill the windscreen and start to gush into the car, then she was jerked sideways and her head smacked into the door pillar. A tunnel of darkness closed in on her, the blow to her head rendering her unconscious.

Chapter Nine

It was a kiss, and a kiss should be something to savour, something that gave great pleasure, something that was exciting, maybe even a bit naughty—but this kiss was rubbish. Agatha had smooched with some really good kissers in her time, but this guy was the pits. What was he doing, trying to eat her alive? And now he was *blowing*! What the hell was that all about?

She opened her eyes to find a stranger leaning over her with his mouth clamped to hers. She squealed in protest, wriggling, thumping, slapping and scuttling away from him.

"Snakes and bastards!" She wiped her mouth on the back of her hand. "Keep away from me, you weirdo!"

"Thank God," the man breathed. "Mrs. Raisin, it's me, PC Hastings . . . Paul."

Agatha stared at him, aghast, then realised that he was soaking wet. Water was dripping off his hair, his black uniform T-shirt and his body armour vest.

"What's going on?" she demanded. "Where am I?" She

cast her eyes from left to right, taking in a riverbank without really registering what she was seeing. Then she realised that she was also soaked to the skin. Her dress had ridden up into an embarrassingly undignified thigh-high rumple, and one of her shoes was missing. She tugged at the hem of the dress but couldn't grip it tightly and it slipped out of her hand. She was confused, and suddenly very angry. "What the hell is going on here?"

"Take it easy, Agatha." The voice was calm and reassuring. Agatha looked up to see Alice Peters now crouching beside her. "Paul pulled you out of your car. You were underwater." Alice pointed to the river near the bridge, where the unrecognisable underside and two rear wheels of Agatha's car were all that was showing above the surface of the fast-flowing river.

"Yes!" Agatha suddenly remembered. "A car kept smashing into me. Ran me off the road. I rolled over and . . . I feel so dizzy."

"You banged your head, Agatha," Alice said gently. "Don't worry, an ambulance is on its way. Paul, did you get the number of the other car?"

"I did," came the reply. "I'll go and call it in." He squelched off up the bank.

"You're lucky it was Paul sitting in the car outside Miss Palmer's house," said Alice. "He took off after you when you came past. I was inside the cottage. If it had been me in the car, I don't know if I would have had the strength to wrench open your door and drag you out in time."

181

"Who did this, Alice?" Agatha gasped, breathing heavily.

"We don't know yet. Don't worry about that now. Just try to stay calm."

"I'll get them." Agatha gave a weak, groaning growl. "I'll get them for this, you see if I don't . . ."

An ambulance arrived in a blaze of lights and sirens, disgorging two green-uniformed paramedics, who rushed down the slope, one carrying a large medical bag.

"She was underwater," Alice explained while the paramedics checked Agatha over. "She doesn't appear to have inhaled water into her lungs. She's been talking and breathing fairly normally, but she's a bit confused and she's had a nasty bump on the head. No other apparent injuries."

"Thanks," said one of the paramedics. "We'll look after her now."

Rain started to fall in huge, summer-warm splashes. Agatha tutted as the paramedics fussed over her, then looked up to see Alice opening an umbrella to protect her.

"Really?" she said, groggily. "I mean, how much wetter can I get?"

Agatha woke in a bed with crisp clean sheets, more pillows than she was accustomed to and no cats demanding to be fed. It was an alien environment, and she felt a sudden sharp longing for the angles of the sloping ceilings, the familiar furniture and the sunlight streaming through the window of her own bedroom at home. She smacked her lips. Her mouth was dry.

"Water?" James was sitting by her bedside holding out a glass to her.

"James . . ." She accepted the glass and took a sip. "Thank you. You're an angel. I'm so glad you're here."

"I'm just glad you got away with no more than a bump on the head." He smiled. "You've been asleep for about three hours. They're going to keep you in overnight. Concussion. They want to keep an eye on you."

"Hey, boss!" Simon stuck his head round the door. "Good to see you awake. Fancy us both being in here at the same time, both with concussion. What are the odds, eh? Hey, this is nice, isn't it? You got your own room. Hello, Mr. Lacey."

Agatha was shocked at the sight of him. It sounded like Simon, but it looked nothing like him. His normally thin, angular face was just as puffy and swollen as before, but the bruising had now taken on a darker colour, forming purple-black rings below his eyes. He also had some kind of white plaster mould over his nose that made it look like a miniature ski jump.

"Simon," she said quietly. "You look awful."

"Thanks, boss." He gave his best attempt at his trademark grin. "You don't look so hot yourself." He was wearing blue pyjamas, and a dark blue dressing gown with a football club badge on the breast pocket. He reached into one of the other pockets and produced a small white paper bag.

"Chocolate raisins," he said. "Best the hospital shop had, and it seemed appropriate."

"Thank you, Simon." Agatha smiled. "I'll try—"

"Agatha! You poor thing! We came as soon as we could!"

Claudette rushed into the room with tears on her cheeks and slipped past Simon to kneel at the opposite side of the bed to James, taking one of Agatha's hands in hers.

"Claudette, you really didn't need to . . ."

"How are you feeling, Agatha? Are you all right?" Pascal stepped into the room. James looked up as he entered, a forlorn expression on his face. He got up, his eyes never leaving the Frenchman.

"I think I had best leave," he said, standing tall and proud.

"Please do not leave on my account," said Pascal. "It is more important that you are here for her."

"Hardly," said James. "You appear to be the important one."

Agatha scowled at them and Simon folded his arms, leaning back against the wall. He wasn't entirely sure what was going on with this apparent stand-off—whether they were each trying to surrender to the other or whether there was about to be a punch-up—but whatever was happening, it was good entertainment.

"Not I." Pascal shook his head. "Why would you say that?"

"Because I saw you together outside The Feathers at lunchtime."

"You saw," Pascal shrugged his shoulders, "but you did not see. She was saying farewell. She sees me only as—"

"She?" Agatha interrupted. "I am still here, you know, still in the room, still alive, still conscious!"

"But of course. Please forgive me." Pascal put his hand on his heart and gave a slight bow. "Agatha would like us to be friends, but there is no more than that for us. She . . ." he nodded again for Agatha's approval, "does not feel for me as she does for you, James. She may like me, but she loves you. A Frenchman would know that," he gave a short laugh, "but you English have not the same madness of romance that afflicts us. Agatha wants to be with you, James, because she loves you."

"So you're saying that was nothing—when I saw the two of you together?"

"Not nothing. It was an ending and a beginning. The end of my hopes and the beginning of what I believe will be a lasting friendship."

"Very well, old boy," said James. His eyes never left the Frenchman as he extended his hand. "If Agatha wants to have you as a friend, then you and I should also be friends."

Pascal shook James's hand. Fresh tears were now coursing down Claudette's face, and Simon was agog.

"Well," said Agatha, folding her arms. "This is all very . . ." she looked towards Simon, "mushy. I need time to think, so why don't you take this little soap opera elsewhere and give me some peace? Go on, off you go, the lot of you. I want some time to myself."

They all trooped out, and once the door closed, Agatha let out a long breath. The exchange between James and Pascal had been excruciating—squirmingly embarrassing. What was wrong with these people? Hospital visits were bad enough—horrible forced conversations where no one knew quite what to say and there were long, awkward silences. That performance, however, had been on a different level completely. It had been hideous. What was wrong with a quick word, a smile and a bunch of grapes? Why did they have to play out an entire drama like that?

She reached for Simon's chocolate raisins and popped a few in her mouth. This was not the sort of thing she normally allowed herself to eat. It wasn't even the sort of thing that she normally enjoyed. Too sweet, too chocolatey, too raisiny—a dieter's nightmare. They must be way off the top of the calorie scale. At this particular moment, however, they were exactly what she wanted—comforting and easy to eat while you were thinking about how everyone around you had gone bonkers. The calories didn't matter anyway. It wasn't as if she was going to have to squeeze into a cocktail dress any time soon, was it? Or try to impress with a posh frock and a ridiculous hat at a high-society garden party—not that she'd be able to wear a hat over the lump on the side of her head, which felt about the size of an ostrich egg. That was the sort of party she might have gone to with Charles. Charles . . . he hadn't even got a mention at the "Pascal and James: Who Does Agatha Love Most?" contest. If he knew how those two had behaved, he'd be laughing his socks off. Little neat socks, ironed by Gustav.

So where *did* Charles fit in? Did he fit in at all, or was he now, like Pascal, a thing of the past? At one time, he had meant far more to her than Pascal, so did Pascal really understand her enough to make pronouncements like "She may like me, but she loves you"? And even in his smooth, chocolatey double bass of a voice, was he right? Did she really love James? Well of course she did, but . . . SNAKES

186

AND BASTARDS! These people were driving her mad! She grabbed another handful of chocolate raisins and stuffed them into her mouth.

She had just gulped down the last of the raisins when there was a knock at the door.

"I thought I told you lot to bug—" Agatha stopped herself as Toni popped her head round the door.

"Hello, Agatha," she smiled. "How are you? I came earlier, but you were sleeping." She produced a small but very pretty bunch of flowers.

"Thank you, Toni," Agatha said, greatly relieved to see that it was her and not part two of the Pascal and James show. "I'm feeling much better, but just like they said about Simon, they're keeping me in overnight. In the morning, I'll be right as rain."

"Well, there's plenty of that at the moment," said Toni. "Rain, I mean. It's been hammering down for hours. Anyway, I thought I'd let you know that I spoke to Paul Hastings, and he says the car that ran you off the road was registered to none other than Harold Nelson."

"It was Nelson's car?" said Agatha. "So Cathy Nelson was driving it?"

"That was what Bill Wong and Alice first thought too, but she couldn't have been driving. Patrick and I were at her block of flats questioning the neighbours when you were run off the road, and I saw her standing on her balcony when we arrived, smoking. She was nowhere near Willow Way, and what's more, she doesn't even drive. She's never sat a test."

"So where does that leave us?" Agatha pondered. "Somebody tried to kill me earlier today, but who? Could somebody think we're getting close to finding out who killed the Admiral and Miss Palmer?"

"But we're not really, are we? What could we have done to make anyone think we were about to expose the murderer?"

"I don't know. Then there's Blackbeard's lot. Bill Wong said I should be on my guard because they'd be after me. Did they try to bump me off using Cathy's car to make it look like it was all mixed up with the Admiral's death?"

"Could be. On the other hand, they'd probably want to advertise that it was them. You know, as a fear thing, to show everyone that they're not to be crossed."

"Maybe . . ." Agatha was feeling tired. "Too many maybes. Let's go over it all in the morning, Toni. I'll go home when I get out of here and freshen up, but I'll be in the office a bit later."

"Are you sure you don't want to take some time off and rest?"

"I'll get some rest now. See you tomorrow."

"Okay . . . and Agatha?"

"Yes?"

"You've got chocolate all round your mouth."

The following morning, James drove Agatha home to Carsely, their conversation during the journey ranging from the bowling green murder and the incessant rain to a return visit to Marco's bistro in Evesham and how much the lump on her head had shrunk. Pascal was not mentioned.

"So your car is a complete write-off," James said, pulling in to Lilac Lane.

"Yes, I suppose I'll have to get a new one." Agatha sighed. "It was leased through Raisin Investigations. I'll need to get in touch with the leasing company."

"Let Helen handle that," James advised. "You should take it easy for a while. I've got this French road trip coming up. Why don't you come with me? Get away from it all for a while?"

"There's no chance of that at the moment, not with a double murder to solve."

Agatha hurried indoors out of the rain, telling James they could talk more later, but without specifying how much later. Later that day, later that week, later that year—all were almost certain. When it came to the scene in the hospital the previous evening, later probably meant never.

Roy Silver was waiting for her indoors, bustling around the kitchen in a flour-dusted apron.

"It's so good to have you home, darling!" he gushed. "I'm baking you a home-coming cake, and we must talk before you rush off again."

Once Agatha had showered, washed the smell of the hospital out of her hair and made herself look presentable, she rejoined Roy in the kitchen.

"I would have come to see you," he said, "but I simply can't stand hospitals."

"Mircester Hospital's not top of my favourite places to

revisit either," Agatha agreed. "So what do you have to tell me?"

"Well, I spent a lot of time at the club yesterday, and I picked up a few things of interest. Stanley Partridge was president before the Admiral—he beat him in the election—and they were sworn enemies. He stopped Nelson getting the presidency that time, but when old Stan's term ended, the Admiral was voted in, and when he started threatening to do away with the rose garden, Stan said he would do away with the Admiral. He said he'd kill him, can you believe that? He's properly passionate about his roses. Then, just a few weeks ago, when the Admiral started trying to round up support to change the rules so that he could be president again, Stan told people he'd 'see the old fraud in his grave' rather than let him do it. That's two death threats!"

"Yes, but people say things like that without really meaning them literally," Agatha pointed out, "and I don't see Stanley Partridge as a murderer, killing for his roses, do you?"

"He loves his roses and he hated the Admiral. Love and hate are things that can drive almost anyone to murder."

"Love and hate," Agatha repeated. "Can't argue with that. Stanley Partridge remains a suspect. I'll ask Patrick to dig into his background. Do you have anything else for me?"

"I do, I do. It seems that seven years ago, the last time Miss Palmer was seen at the club, she was in a real state. It was just after the Admiral announced he was going to marry Cathy. She was yelling about stopping the wedding and that it was unlawful and against God. The Swinburns calmed her down. They told her to be patient and that everything would work itself out.

"When the Admiral became president, it was Mrs. Swinburn who lost to him. There were only a few votes in it, and some said the Admiral had somehow managed to rig the result. He got his three years in charge, but it wasn't a happy time. Some members left because of his bullying and nastiness. He was livid when they rejoined shortly before the last election and helped to vote in Mrs. Swinburn. He had wanted to put one of his cronies in charge."

"I'd already heard that he wanted to change the rules so that he could become president again," said Agatha.

"Not just president again," Roy corrected her. "President for *life*."

"You can see how that might tip someone over the edge," said Patrick, listening to Agatha report Roy's findings. He was sitting with his back to his desk, sipping coffee and discussing the case with Agatha and Toni, both of whom had taken seats in Raisin Investigations' main office. "I'd say that makes Stanley Partridge a suspect, along with the Swinburns."

"What about the neighbour Nelson had a fight with?" Agatha asked.

"A retired gardener," said Patrick. "He denied killing the Admiral, but said he was glad he was dead. No love lost there. He has no alibi for the time of the murder."

"He would have known about the weedkiller being a

deadly poison, and he could have stolen the Admiral's car," Toni added. "Cathy Nelson says someone must have taken it and then put it back. She was out on the balcony for a smoke when she saw it in the car park looking all bashed up. She was furious because she had been intending to sell it, so she went down to take a look. That was the first time she had gone near the car in weeks."

"I've been thinking about that," said Agatha. "Just because she hasn't passed a driving test and doesn't have a licence doesn't mean she can't drive. You saw her on the balcony when you arrived, Toni, but that doesn't mean she was in her flat all the time you and Patrick were knocking on doors. She could have sneaked out and driven the car to run me off the road because she thought we were getting too close to her."

"Why would she then park the damaged car back in its space outside the flats?" Patrick asked. "Surely she'd want to ditch it somewhere."

"But she knew the car had been seen chasing Agatha," said Toni, "and by a police officer, no less. Maybe bringing it back was a double bluff so that she could get home, claim to have been there all afternoon and say that someone stole the car and was trying to make it look like she ran Agatha into the river."

"Anything's possible," Agatha sighed, touching the bump on her head. "All this thinking's making my head ache." She jumped as the phone on the desk rang. "Good morning, Raisin Investigations." She immediately covered the mouthpiece. "Speak of the devil," she hissed to the others. "It's Cathy Nelson!"

Toni and Patrick listened in silence to the one-sided conversation.

"Yes, I see," said Agatha. "You've not been charged with anything and the police are investigating further. So you're at home. Well, I'm a bit busy this afternoon and the funeral's tomorrow, isn't it? You want us to come and see you tomorrow afternoon? Very well, if you insist."

She ended the call and looked across at her assistant. "Dig out your best black dress tonight, Toni. We're going to a funeral. In the meantime, I've arranged for us to drop in on a young lady in Herris."

Philippa Miller lived in a semi-detached cottage similar to Miss Palmer's but far less isolated, in the heart of Herris Cum Magna. Like Ancombe, Herris was the kind of chocolate-box-pretty Cotswold village that had helped to turn the region into an Area of Outstanding Natural Beauty and a major tourist attraction.

Toni pulled into the small parking space to the side of the front garden and Miss Miller opened the front door to greet them. She was a vivacious young woman with bright eyes and a ready smile. She introduced them to Sam, the cosily wrapped bundle of baby she was carrying, and invited them in. They sat in her front room, a comfortable space decorated in a more modern style than Agatha felt suited the house. The decor, however, made the child's play mat, with its bridge of dangling toys, and all of the other colorful baby paraphernalia seem entirely at home.

"Let me make us some coffee." Miss Miller approached Agatha and, before she could utter a word of protest, nestled the baby in her lap. "You don't mind, do you? It's just that I don't want to let him sleep yet and I want him to get used to meeting different people."

Agatha nodded and put an arm round the baby, who looked up at her expectantly, although neither of them had any inkling what he might be expecting. Not knowing what else to do, she smiled at him, he smiled back and they became instant friends, much to Toni's amusement. By the time Miss Miller returned, the baby was in Toni's arms, concentrating intently on gripping one of Toni's thumbs in both his hands.

"Thank you for seeing us, Miss Miller," said Agatha.

"Please, just call me Philippa." Miss Miller retrieved her son and sat with him cradled in her arm. "So you want to talk to me about Rupert?"

"Yes," said Agatha, "and little Sam."

"Rupert's saying Sam's not his and wants you to prove it." Miss Miller cut straight to the point.

"Quite right," Agatha agreed. "He seems to think you're—"

"A gold digger who's after his money," said Miss Miller.

"That's not exactly how I would have put it," Agatha said.

"Of course you wouldn't, Mrs. Raisin," Miss Miller agreed. "I wouldn't expect you to, but I know who you are. Agatha Raisin, PR guru turned private eye. I knew when you called that we would be able to understand each other, so I know you'll believe me when I tell you that I don't want any money from that chinless prat Rupert Ferrington-Slade. I work in marketing. I own this house. I have a solid career and I will provide for my son out of my own pocket."

"So why does Mr. Ferrington-Slade think he's being set up?"

"You'd have to ask him that," said Miss Miller, gently tickling her baby's nose. "All I want is for my little Sammy to know who his daddy is. Rupert might not want to recognise Sam, but one day Sam will ask, and he has a right to know."

"Mr. Ferrington-Slade denies that Sam is his," said Agatha.

"Get him to submit to a DNA test." Miss Miller handed Agatha an envelope. "This is the result of Sam's. It might be useful to you."

"It might indeed," Agatha agreed, accepting the envelope. "But tell me, if you don't want money, is there something else you want? Marriage maybe?"

"Marry *him*? Don't make me laugh. He was fun at parties for a while, and he can be a real charmer when he wants to, but I wouldn't want to marry him. That would be a disaster."

"So the baby was a mistake?" asked Toni.

"Oh, don't say that." Miss Miller hugged her baby close and kissed his head. "Sam's my little miracle, aren't you, Sammy? Yes, you're gorgeous, aren't you? Such a handsome boy!"

They said their goodbyes, leaving Philippa showering Sam with a mother's love.

"He was a beautiful baby, wasn't he?" Toni said as they got into the car.

"Oh dear, Toni," Agatha smiled, teasing her. "You're too young to be getting broody."

"It's not that," Toni laughed, pulling out onto the road. "It's just that, well, Philippa obviously adores that little boy. It's almost unfair the way some children are born to have loving, caring parents and some will never know that special bond."

"You mean like you and me, with our parents?"

"Yes . . . and perhaps the baby that Constance was forced to give up all those years ago."

"That baby may have gone to a loving home for all we know. It almost certainly went to a better home than the Admiral would ever have given it. He absolutely hated children."

"How can you hate a baby like little Sam? I mean, he was just so cute."

"Don't let that broody thing take hold, Toni. After all, there's no prospect of your own little Sam at the moment, is there? You are footloose and fancy free, as you put it. No boyfriend on the horizon."

"That's not entirely true any more," Toni said coyly.

"Really?" Agatha sat up and stared at her. "Do tell. Who is this mystery guy?"

"You know him, actually." Toni glanced at her warily. "Paul asked me out—Paul Hastings. I'm seeing him tomorrow night."

"PC Hastings?" Agatha sounded horrified. "The infamous Paul Easeman? How could you, Toni? That's not how to play the game. We're supposed to be thinking of ways to get our revenge on him, ways to win. Now, instead of him coming last, you're offering him the star prize!"

"But Agatha . . ." Toni looked across at her boss, and Agatha gave her a huge, beaming smile. Toni let out a sigh of relief. "You're just winding me up."

"And you took the bait beautifully." Agatha laughed. "I can't really hold anything against that young man any more, can I? He saved my life, after all, and he seems very nice."

"He is. He's really nice, and anyway . . ." Toni shifted her shoulders in a perky wiggle, "I think I quite like the idea of being a star prize!"

"It's just as well I didn't get my own back on him then," Agatha said. "Then you'd have been the booby prize!"

The Admiral's funeral took place the following morning at Mircester Crematorium. The building was modern, functional and spartan, the formal flower beds outside laid in regimented rows and planted with respectful roses in a solemn dark red, the blooms nodding under the onslaught of yet another heavy rain shower. Agatha and Toni joined the mourners, mainly members of the Mircester Crown Green Bowling Club, filing in to pay their last respects. Many were dressed in dark blue blazers and bowling whites, but with black ties or armbands. Most of the ladies wore sombre black. Agatha generally preferred colours that suited the season, suited her character or suited her mood, but when trying on her black dress that morning, she had been pleasantly surprised to see how much slimmer it made her look. She sighed at the wasted effect. Looking good at a funeral probably wasn't going to win her any admirers.

The mourners filed past the open coffin where the Admiral lay dressed, like so many of the mourners, in his blue blazer and bowls attire. His grey hair was tidy and his beard had been trimmed. Make-up successfully disguised the ravages that a lifetime of booze had taken on his face, and Agatha mentally congratulated the undertakers on making him look so much better than he had done the last time she had seen him—so much better, she guessed, than the last time anyone had seen him alive.

They listened to an overly flattering eulogy delivered by a religiously neutral funeral celebrant who clearly had no idea who the Admiral was, watched the now-closed coffin disappear silently on muffled electric rollers through a velvet curtain, then queued to nod and shake hands with Cathy Nelson on the way out.

"Give me a couple of hours to sort out the formalities and get rid of this lot," Cathy whispered to Agatha, "then meet me back at my flat. I've got something to show you."

Agatha and Toni trotted down the steps in the grassy embankment leading to the main door of Cathy Nelson's apartment block. They sheltered beneath umbrellas until they were inside the entrance hall, then collapsed and shook them to get rid of the excess water as they waited for the lift. The lift, however, failed to appear. According to the indicator lights, it was stubbornly stuck on the second floor.

"Come on, Toni," said Agatha, turning towards the stairwell. "We're fit enough to climb a couple of flights."

They hurried up the stairs, and on reaching the second floor, Toni turned right.

"Mrs. Nelson's flat is this way, isn't it?" she said.

Agatha nodded, unwilling to talk lest it show how hard she was breathing.

"Look," Toni pointed, "the door's not properly closed."

"That's strange." Agatha had now recovered enough to speak, and pushed the door wide open. "Hello? Mrs. Nelson? Anyone home?"

There was no response, so the two women made their way inside. The heavy rain clouds had made the flat quite dark, and there were lights on in the short hall and the sitting room. Laid out on the coffee table, Agatha could see the documents that Mrs. Nelson had concealed during their previous visit.

"Check the other rooms, Toni." As she flicked through the pages, her hand nudged against one of two cigarette packs on the table. It rattled. Curious, she picked them both up. One was almost full with cigarettes; the other had nothing in it but a small gold lapel badge. The Admiral's president's badge, Agatha mused. Was that a strange thing for Cathy Nelson to keep? Maybe she wanted to sell it. It was gold, after all, but quite small and not worth very much. And why hide it away in an empty cigarette packet?

She returned to the documents, which included a handwritten letter from Cathy Nelson to a company called Ancestry Tracer and a report the company had prepared for her. What she saw in the report left her startled.

"No sign of her anywhere," Toni reported. "What's that on the mantelpiece?"

Agatha turned and picked up an envelope on which was printed—clearly from a computer printer rather than an old Remington like Miss Palmer's—the words *To Whom It May Concern*.

"That could be us." She shrugged and opened the envelope. An old, faded black and white photograph fell out. Toni picked it up.

"Wow," she said, studying the couple in the photo. The man was dressed in the Royal Navy uniform of an able-bodied seaman and the woman wore a plain white wedding dress. "Look at that young guy—it's the Admiral. This photo must be from his first wedding. She looks like a young Cathy Nelson, doesn't she?"

"That's poor Constance," said Agatha, pulling a folded sheet of paper from the envelope. She opened it and read out the words: "I am glad he is dead! He killed my mother! He was evil! He knew! He knew—and now everyone else will, too. I can't bear the shame. I hope he rots in hell!"

"Cathy Nelson was tracing the Admiral's family history," she nodded at the documents on the table, "and her own. They extracted DNA from the samples she sent and it turned out that Cathy was actually his daughter. The bastard married his own daughter!"

"Agatha—this is a suicide note!"

The curtains by the full-length window billowed in a sudden gust of wind, and they realised for the first time that the window was open. They rushed to the balcony. Below them on the ground, face down on the embankment, lay Cathy Nelson.

"Call an ambulance!" Agatha yelled, dashing for the door.

Chapter Ten

The main bar area of the Mircester Crown Green Bowling Club smelled of fresh paint and linoleum polish. The doors to the veranda that overlooked the bowling green stood open to allow a free flow of fresh air, and from where she sat, Agatha could see the emerald and jade stripes of the precisely mown playing surface luxuriating in the sunshine, the rain clouds having drifted off to the east. To her right was a bar, currently dormant and in darkness behind a closed metal grille, and to her left, on the other side of the clubhouse lounge, was the door to the kitchen and a serving hatch, both also closed. She sat at a table with Mr. and Mrs. Swinburn, the elderly couple hugely apologetic for not being able to offer her tea.

"The kitchen's all locked up, you see," said Mr. Swinburn. "The renovation team have the keys, and of course, the bar is closed at this time of day."

"That's not a problem," Agatha said. "Thank you for agreeing to see me here."

"It's our pleasure, dear," said Mrs. Swinburn. "It gave us a chance to open the doors and air the place now that the rain has stopped. What did you want to talk to us about? Have you any news about the Admiral's killer?"

"There is certainly some news," Agatha agreed, "and I'm afraid it's not good."

"Really?" said Mrs. Swinburn. "What on earth has happened?"

"Well . . . Oh, Mrs. Swinburn, what happened to your gold badge?" Agatha pointed to the pin-hole mark on the old lady's lapel.

"I think it fell off in the car," Mrs. Swinburn explained, stroking the blank space. "The seat belt, you know? It rubs against my shoulder. We haven't found it yet."

"Could be a job for the lads down at our old workshop," said Mr. Swinburn. "They might have to take out the seats."

"Oh dear," said Agatha. "Good luck with that. So . . . what I wanted to tell you was that yesterday afternoon, Cathy Nelson's body was found at her block of flats, beneath her balcony. I was there with a colleague and it was us who found her. She was still wearing her black dress from the funeral. It looked like suicide."

"Suicide? Oh my goodness!" Mrs. Swinburn held her husband's hand and waited for more.

"It seems that Mrs. Nelson was trying to trace her husband's ancestry to find out if, as he often claimed, he was related to Admiral Lord Horatio Nelson. She sent off a sample, from which they extracted his DNA. At the same time, she had her DNA sampled to trace her own roots. Lots of people do this nowadays. It's very popular.

"The results showed that Harry Nelson was not related

203

to Horatio Nelson, but that he *was* related to Cathy Nelson. He was her *father.* She was the child that his first wife, Constance, gave up for adoption before they were married. We found a photograph of Harry and Connie on their wedding day, and the likeness between Cathy and her mother was unmistakable."

"Well, I never," Mr. Swinburn breathed.

"So now Cathy, something of an orphan and a drifter all her life, knew who her mother was. She also realised that the stories she had heard about Harry having killed his first wife meant that he had murdered her mother. The wedding photograph she discovered showed that she was the spitting image of her mother, too. Now she could see that Harry must have known who she was from the moment he first saw her. He knew she was his daughter and he married her to keep her close, to make sure that she would do what he thought a daughter should—look after her father in his old age."

"The poor woman must have been beside herself!" Mrs. Swinburn gasped.

"I'd say she was distraught, and I'd say she was furious," said Agatha. "Angry enough, I'd guess, to kill Harry Nelson in order to avenge the mother she never knew and to avenge herself for the shame he'd caused her by tricking her into marrying her own father."

"He was a wicked, wicked man." Mr. Swinburn shook his head in disgust.

"She mixed his painkillers with some of his Smuggler's Breath rum here at the club, and when he gulped it down, he became so stupefied that it was easy to mix half a bottle of his weedkiller with more rum and let him drink that, too. That's why, despite the fact that Harry always used a full bottle of weedkiller on the paths—that was his measure—there was a half-full bottle on the shelf in the tool shed.

"Sadly, the story doesn't end there, because Miss Palmer, just as Harry had done, had recognised who Cathy was straight away. She was appalled by the illegal, immoral marriage and it tormented her for years. Should she denounce the Admiral and let the world know what he had done? He would surely be punished, but Cathy would suffer more. She would suffer the disgrace, and Miss Palmer was loath to inflict that on her. When Harry was killed, however, the situation changed. She couldn't keep quiet when she suspected that he had been murdered.

"Cathy must have realised that Miss Palmer was on the verge of exposing the whole sordid business, and killed her, too. Then, when she thought I was getting close, I was the next one she tried to bump off. After the funeral, she realised that the truth was going to come out and it all got too much for her, so she wrote a suicide note and threw herself out of the window, just as people believed her mother had done all those years ago."

"That's such a dreadfully sad story," Mrs. Swinburn said with a sob, dabbing a tissue to her eye.

"It is," Agatha nodded, "but it's not entirely true, is it?"

"What do you mean?" Mr. Swinburn frowned.

"Well, the suicide note got me thinking," Agatha explained. "It was a bit hysterical and didn't really sound like the Cathy Nelson I had spoken to. She would have been mortified by the whole situation, naturally, but she had always been a drifter. She had no roots in Mircester and nothing to stay here for. She could simply have sold up and moved on, far more financially secure than ever before.

'The note was also produced on a computer and printed out. Cathy had neither a computer nor a printer. She could have gone to an internet café to do it, but that's hardly likely, is it? No, if she was to leave a suicide note, it would have been hand-written and signed, so I came to the conclusion that the printed, unsigned note was a forgery. That being the case, the death of Cathy Nelson was more likely to be murder than suicide, but who killed her?

"Then I found this." Agatha produced a cigarette packet from her handbag and emptied out the small gold president's badge onto the table. "It's yours, isn't it, Mrs. Swinburn?"

"It might be," said the old woman. "Where did you find it?"

"I didn't," Agatha admitted. "Cathy Nelson did. When she looked down from her balcony the day my car was forced into the river and saw Harry's car so badly damaged, I'd say she was livid. She'd planned to sell the thing, but now it was worth practically nothing. She went down to take a look at it and found this on the floor. You lost your badge in a car, Mrs. Swinburn, but not in your own car; in Harry Nelson's car when you two were trying to murder me."

"That's ridiculous!" barked Mr. Swinburn. "That could be any past president's badge!"

206

"The only other past president on our suspect list is Mr. Partridge, and he showed me his badge earlier this morning. We checked the other living former presidents, of course. There aren't many, and they all have their badges."

"If Cathy had that thing, it must be the Admiral's badge!" cried Mrs. Swinburn.

"That's what I thought," said Agatha. "Then I realised that his went into the furnace on the lapel of his blazer. I'm betting that the only fingerprints on this badge are Cathy Nelson's and yours, Mrs. Swinburn."

"Fingerprints?" His face crimson with anger, Mr. Swinburn grabbed the badge and rubbed his own fingers all over it. "What fingerprints? You can't prove any of this! You've no evidence at all!"

"If I look hard enough, I will find the evidence," Agatha promised, "because it all fits. Cathy Nelson told me that you visited her shortly after her husband's death. I'm betting that one of you used the bathroom and planted the painkillers in the cabinet. Cathy said she'd never seen them before and Harry had no history of needing painkillers, but you knew you'd have to subdue him in order to get him to drink the poisoned rum, and the mixture of alcohol and the powerful drugs did the trick. But you also knew the pathologist would find traces of the painkillers, so you had to make it look like they were Harry's.

"Had everyone believed that Harry committed suicide, you would have been happy, but then I started shouting about murder, and people read about it in the *Telegraph*. That didn't concern you too much, though, because you had already put a backup plan in place. It was you who suggested to Cathy Nelson that she should contact Ancestry Tracer in order to stop Harry from shouting his mouth off about being related to Admiral Nelson. You also encouraged her to give it a go herself. You knew what she would find out. As soon as you heard that the information had arrived, you went ahead with the murder. You provided her with a powerful motive so that the finger of blame would point to her, leaving you two in the clear."

"You have no way of knowing if that's true or not." Mr. Swinburn now seemed to have calmed down and appeared coolly confident. "You're guessing."

"Okay, how's this for a guess?" Agatha shrugged. "I think you're the ones who persuaded Miss Palmer to keep the scandal of the Nelsons' marriage under her hat. Maybe you told her that you would take care of it all. Maybe you thought you could use that secret to have the Admiral booted out of your precious bowls club. But it all came to a head when he started talking about becoming president for life. You simply couldn't allow that to happen. You hated him for all the disruption he was threatening at the club you both so love, but the hatred runs far deeper than that, doesn't it?

"You told me about your business, and about selling up when you retired—not passing on the business to your children. That's because you've never been able to have children, have you? When Harry Nelson abandoned Constance with a baby on the way, you must have been appalled."

"We'd have taken that baby," Mrs. Swinburn's voice was wavering. "We'd have given it a loving home and a good life, but it had to be sent away. It couldn't be raised locally. That might have caused problems."

"And when Constance died with another baby on the way," Agatha continued, "that must have hit you hard, too."

"We knew he did it." Mr. Swinburn's voice was hard. "We were certain he killed her. He was a vile human being. Not a human being—an animal."

"Back to your business, Mr. Swinburn," Agatha went on. "Auto repairs. You know your way around cars. It must have been easy for you to steal Harry Nelson's old car to use as a battering ram against me. I should think it was even easier for you to steal the car you used to kill Miss Palmer."

"That car was set alight—there was practically nothing left of it," Mr. Swinburn said. "No proof that we had anything to do with it."

"The Admiral's murder was too much for Miss Palmer. You knew she'd talk. The case was closed as far as the police were concerned—an accident—but you saw her speaking to me at the ladies' society talk, didn't you, Mrs. Swinburn? So you had to stop her from telling me everything. How could you do that? How could you murder a woman you had known almost all your lives?"

"She was going to ruin everything!" Mr. Swinburn snapped.

"Charlie, bite your tongue," warned Mrs. Swinburn. "You've said enough!"

"She's got nothing, my dear. She'll never prove any of

this," Mr. Swinburn sneered. "Dorothy Palmer was a silly old fool. We sent her to her God in heaven and I hope she's at peace. And Harry Nelson? I hope we sent him to the other place. You got off lightly, but you need to drop this now or next time maybe you won't be so lucky. You can't prove we killed Harry or Dorothy and you can't prove we killed Cathy."

"You haven't been very careful so far," Agatha goaded him. "You didn't realise that Cathy Nelson couldn't drive, did you? Miss Palmer's death, and my death for that matter, could never have been blamed on her. So many mistakes. Once the police forensics people get to work in her flat, I'm sure they'll find bits and pieces to place you at the scene.

"Maybe you left fingerprints on the Admiral's old wedding photograph. That's not the sort of thing he would have kept. You gave it to Cathy, didn't you? Or maybe they'll find the key you had made to let yourself into her flat yesterday. How did you get that? Secretly take an impression of her house key during your little visit, perhaps?"

"No need." Smugness and overconfidence gave way to recklessness, and Mr. Swinburn pulled a key ring from his pocket. "The Admiral's house keys and car keys were left lying around. All I had to do was pocket them. It couldn't have been easier."

"Yesterday afternoon was tricky, though, wasn't it? I think you were still there when Toni and I arrived. You're not good with stairs, Mrs. Swinburn, so you stopped the lift on the second floor to make sure you could get out quickly. That's why Toni and I had to use the stairs. You bundled Cathy off the balcony while we were waiting for the lift. By the time we got upstairs, you were on your way down. We must have missed each other by seconds.

"I reckon you were sheltering somewhere near the main entrance, watching for Cathy to come out onto the balcony for a smoke. Then you hurried inside, took the lift, let yourselves in and crept up behind her. It took both of you to heave her off the balcony, and we know for a fact that Cathy was attacked by two people. Although she can't remember much about what happened, she is certain about that."

"Wait a minute . . . Cathy's certain?" Mrs. Swinburn sounded confused. "You mean she's—"

"Roy!" Agatha called, and the kitchen serving hatch was flung open. Standing in the kitchen, framed in the hatch, were Roy Silver, Toni and, wearing a neck brace and her arm in a sling, Cathy Nelson. "My friend Roy has been working with your renovations team. He had the keys to let the others in."

"And I think I've heard all I need to," said Bill Wong, walking in through the kitchen door. Alice Peters and PC Hastings appeared on the veranda. Mrs. Swinburn burst into tears. Her husband put his arm around her.

"All the rain we've had turned the grass embankment at the front of the building as soft as a mattress. Cathy has a lot of bruising, plenty of aches and pains and a couple of broken bones, but she's far from dead," Agatha explained as Cathy Nelson hobbled into the room, supporting herself with a walking stick in her free hand. "Had it not been so wet, you'd be facing a third murder charge. As it is, you'll be spending the rest of your lives in jail."

Bill placed the Swinburns under arrest and they were led out of the club, their heads bowed.

"Thank you, Mrs. Raisin." Cathy Nelson lowered herself carefully into a seat, Toni hovering at her elbow to help if needed. "This has all been a complete nightmare."

"I can well believe that," Agatha sympathised. "What will you do now? Will you sell the flat and move on?"

"No, I don't think so." Cathy sounded positive. "None of this was my fault. I know there will be gossip, but I can cope with that. I don't see why I should run away. This isn't a bad place to live, after all. Maybe when I'm better, I might even take up bowls!"

Later that afternoon, Agatha and Toni arrived at The Beeches, a development of modern homes almost hidden from the rest of suburban Mircester by screens of carefully planted fir trees. Toni parked the car outside a house with a front garden consisting of a neat square of lawn and regimented flower borders with pink and white geraniums and fuchsias standing obediently on parade. Although each of the houses in the close was slightly different, the front gardens, with their short driveways leading to identical garages, were indistinguishable. It was a place, Agatha decided, that might have been built as some kind of bizarre scientific experiment and inhabited by human clones, or androids, or insurance salesmen.

"Wait here, will you, Toni?" she said. "I won't be long."

She pushed open the front gate with its wooden sign announcing the house as "Clarendon" and pressed the doorbell. Electronic chimes clanged out a furious rendition of "Rule Britannia," and the door was opened by a large woman with an irritated scowl on her face.

"Hello, Mrs. Wong." Agatha smiled.

"What do you want?" Bill's mother grumbled. "Bill's not here."

"I know that," said Agatha, ignoring the woman's rudeness, determined not to deviate from her charm offensive. "It's you and Mr. Wong I've come to see."

"Who is it, Mother?" came a voice from the sitting room.

"It's that Raisin woman!" yelled Mrs. Wong.

"Tell her we're not in!"

"It's a bit late for that really, isn't it?" Agatha kept her smile on full beam.

"This is Father's day off." Mrs. Wong's voice was sullen. "Father watches the horses on his day off. You can't disturb his racing."

"I won't take up much of his time, but this is important, Mrs. Wong," Agatha said. "It's about Bill."

Realising that she wasn't going to get rid of her visitor, Mrs. Wong gave a deep sigh, opened the door wide and turned her back, lumbering off towards the living room. Agatha followed. The room was every bit as chintzy as she remembered from her previous visits. The carpet was an eye-wateringly pink shag pile and the three-piece suite had protective plastic coverings on the arms and backs. She had suffered Mrs. Wong's cooking with both Charles and James on separate occasions in this house and had promised herself she would never return. But now here she was, transfixed by the stuffed parrot sitting on its perch in the corner of the room.

"Five minutes," said Mrs. Wong. "That's when the next race starts."

Agatha tore her eyes away from the parrot and looked towards Mr. Wong, who pressed a button on his remote control to mute the TV. His moustache was a little more grey than she remembered, his pot belly a little rounder, his cardigan more stained and ratty. Only his tartan slippers were the same.

"Five minutes," he grunted.

Agatha sat on the sofa, uninvited. As she leant on the arm, her elbow shot sideways. She straightened up and embarked on the speech she had been rehearsing in her head since lunchtime.

"I seem to have been dealing with a lot of family problems recently," she said, "and I wanted to talk to both of you because, well, the one thing we have in common is your son, Bill. We all care about him and I know that he adores you. That's why we can't let a family problem blight his life."

"No family problems here," mumbled Mr. Wong. "Are there, Mother?"

"No family problems in this house," Mrs. Wong agreed.

"Well, there will be," Agatha warned. "In fact, there are already. I know you persuaded Bill to give up his flat and come back to live with you. I also know that when he marries Alice, you want to try to force them both to live here with you."

"Bill will need to save up for a house," said Mrs. Wong. "Cheaper for us all to live together."

"That's not why you want him here at all, is it?" Agatha shook her head. "You just don't want to let him go, and if that causes a rift between him and Alice, then as far as you're concerned, she's not right for him—not right for you, more like."

Mr. Wong shifted uncomfortably and Mrs. Wong lowered her bulky frame onto the protective plastic of the second armchair.

"I know you think Bill will give up the police one day and come to work with you, Mr. Wong, but that's never going to happen. Apart from anything else, he earns far more as a detective sergeant than you do from your dry-cleaning shop. I know—we've run a business assessment on your place. As a couple, Bill and Alice earn more than twice what you do. They can already afford their own home and you need to let them do that. You need to let them build their own life. You've driven other girls away in the past, but this time, you risk driving Bill away as well."

"You're talking rubbish!" said Mrs. Wong.

"Rubbish!" her husband agreed.

'Am I? Think back, both of you. You know how family rifts develop. What did your family think when you started

215

seeing your wife, Mr. Wong? They weren't happy that you'd taken up with an English girl, were they? They wanted you to marry a nice Chinese girl.

"And you had much the same family problem, didn't you, Mrs. Wong? Your parents didn't want you being with a young Chinese man, did they? So you two struck out on your own—a brave thing to do—and you've had no real contact with your families since."

Agatha's phone rang and she retrieved it from her handbag.

"Hmph!" snorted Mr. Wong. "Now she's taking calls in our house!"

"I've been waiting for this call, but it's not for me, Mr. Wong." Agatha turned the phone's screen to face him. "It's a video call for you. Recognise him? It's your father in Hong Kong."

Mr. Wong's mouth fell open and he stared at the screen. There was a burst of rapid-fire Chinese from the phone, and he took it from Agatha's hand, his eyes fixed on his father's image. He responded with a few words in Chinese, and after a few seconds, Agatha saw, for the first time ever, a smile on his face. A moment later, there was a tear on his cheek. Mrs. Wong looked amazed.

Agatha reached into her handbag again. "Take a look at this picture, Mrs. Wong." She handed over a small photo in a grey cardboard frame. It showed a young girl with blonde hair smiling with pride, dressed in a university graduation gown and holding a diploma.

"That's . . . that's my sister!" Mrs. Wong gasped. "But she never went to university."

"Your sister didn't," Agatha agreed, "but that's not your sister—it's your niece. You've never met her, but she's almost as old as Bill and is now a doctor. She wants to meet you. Your sister wants to see you again, too, and the whole family wants to meet Bill. You two are all the family Bill has ever known, but he deserves to know his other relatives. It's time to let bygones be bygones.

"Give Bill the space he needs to live his own life, or he will end up doing what you did and walk away."

Agatha stood and accepted her phone from Mr. Wong, the screen now blank, the call ended. Bill's parents looked up at her, not uttering a word.

"Think about it," she said, "then do the right thing."

Agatha hurried back to the car, where Toni was waiting patiently.

"How did it go?" she asked.

"Better than I thought." Agatha sounded relieved. "It's up to them now."

"Okay." Toni started the engine. "Do you still want to do this next visit today?"

"No time like the present," said Agatha. "Barfield House, please, Toni."

Agatha sat opposite Charles at his ornate desk in the library at Barfield House, sipping tea reluctantly delivered in an offhand manner by Gustav shortly before they saw him rushing past the terrace windows wearing his yellow hard hat.

"He's busy," said Agatha, "but he loves this house. He must be enjoying overseeing the work that's going on."

"He is." Charles smiled. "The old place was desperately in need of some TLC."

"I saw all the scaffolding," Agatha said. "It must be costing a fortune."

"It is," Charles sighed, "and the cash injection that came from my marriage won't last forever. The estate has to earn more. That's why I want to get the vineyard business up and running, and why I was glad that Rupert suddenly got in touch. He's an investor, lots of money, family backing."

"You might not be so keen on old Rupert when you hear what I've got to tell you." Agatha placed her cup back in its saucer. "He was using you, Charles, and trying to use me. He wanted us to find the father of Philippa Miller's baby, and I think any potential candidate would have done. We did a bit of digging into his situation, you see, and it would appear that this isn't the first paternity suit he's had to deal with. At least three other young women have been paid off by the family, and Rupert was on his last warning—if it happened again, he was to be cut off without a penny. No more family backing to play with. No more income at all."

"He swore the child could not possibly be his." Charles looked stern. "Have you found out who the father is?"

"Oh, it's Rupert's child all right." Agatha sounded positive. "The DNA proves that. It's a harsh and brutal thing, DNA. It tells the truth whether you want to hear it or not."

"But Rupert wouldn't submit to a DNA test," said Charles.

Agatha produced a plastic evidence bag containing a crumpled tissue and held it up for Charles to see.

"I collected one of these off the floor when I was last here," she explained. "I wasn't about to waste my time running around chasing my tail without having eliminated the most obvious suspect first. The baby is his. The only good news for him is that Philippa doesn't want his family's money, so maybe they'll go easy on him this time."

"Well, I won't," said Charles, grimly. "Everyone will know what a swine he is by the time I'm finished."

"You'll lose your investor," Agatha warned.

"He's not the sort I want to do business with," Charles replied. "There are other investors—and some things are more important than money. I . . . I heard about you ending up in the river," he added. "You must have been terrified. I was worried about you. I came to the hospital, but I was told you had just flung out all your visitors and you were sleeping. I waited, but—"

"I know," Agatha said. "They told me you had been. It was sweet of you to come."

"Well," Charles rubbed his hands and smiled, "in lieu of a visit, how about dinner? James too, of course. Let's push the boat out. It'll be just like old times."

"Maybe not quite like old times," she smiled, standing to leave, "but that would be nice. Now I must go. I've left Toni outside. I'm using the poor girl like a taxi service."

219

Charles escorted her to the front door, then stood awkwardly, as if unsure what to say or do. His arm moved as though he were about to shake her hand. She put a hand on his arm, leaned forward and kissed him on the cheek.

"I . . . I've been wanting to build bridges . . ." he said.

"Consider a bridge built." She smiled. "I don't want to end up in a river again any time soon!"

"Was it really necessary to get up quite so early?" Agatha yawned, staring out of the car window at a morning that was still struggling to get off the starting blocks.

"Early?" James laughed, pulling out of the hotel car park. "Dawn was just after five. It's now nearly six. If I'm to supply photographs to accompany the story of this road trip, I want to start with sunrise over the white cliffs of Dover on the first morning."

"I know," Agatha stifled another yawn, "and it's a nice idea."

"The rest of the day will be more relaxing," James promised. "We're on the first ferry out of Newhaven to Dieppe, and then we simply wander down through France to the Med. I'm so glad you're coming with me. You need this time away from work."

"I think I probably do," Agatha agreed. "It's been pretty hectic of late."

"Whatever happened to Cindy Snakehips?" James asked.

"I wondered how long it would take you to ask about her." Agatha laughed. "Miss Higginbotham resigned from her job in the warehouse. It seems she heard that two women from a talent agency visited Shirley's Girlies, and decided to sign up to an agency herself. She now has so many bookings for her act that she's concentrating entirely on what she apparently refers to as her 'stage career.' She'll be travelling all over the country."

"Good for her. Do you think *our* travels might take us to Bordeaux?" said James. "I hear the wine at Chateau Duvivier is particularly fine."

"Why not?" replied Agatha. "They are good friends, after all."

"They are," James nodded.

"Did you see that?" Agatha said suddenly. "Just back there. That green Land Rover."

"Calm down, my dear," James said gently. "You've been seeing green Land Rovers from the time we left The Red Lion in Carsely to when we checked in at The White Lion in Seaford. There are a lot of them about."

They headed down to the seafront, passing Seaford's Martello tower, which James explained was "an intriguing circular fort" built in the first decade of the nineteenth century as one of a chain of gun emplacements designed to defend Britain against invasion by Napoleon. In the watery grey light of dawn, the lone cannon mounted on the roof of the building looked to Agatha like the handle on the lid of a gigantic white casserole pot. Beyond the tower, they found a parking space at the shingle beach near the base of a path that meandered uphill onto the cliffs. The top of the path disappeared into a haze of mist.

221

"That's where we're heading." James looked across at Agatha and raised an eyebrow. "Sensible shoes?"

"Don't worry, I've come prepared for anything," said Agatha. "These are the same shoes I wore for our quokka hunt." She opened the car door, retrieving her pink handbag from the footwell.

"You might as well leave that in the car," said James. "You won't be needing it."

"Even after all these years," Agatha sighed, stepping out of the car with her handbag, "you still know nothing about women, do you?"

Heading up onto the cliff path, Agatha plucked her sunglasses from a jacket pocket. She was squinting against the sunlight, which was startlingly bright when it broke through the thin mist yet still dazzling when the mist closed in as it seemed to bounce around inside the haze, reflecting unpredictably from almost every direction. The sunglasses defended not only against the glare, but also against the squint wrinkles she could feel forming. She knew they'd be there to stay if she gave them the chance.

The mist became increasingly patchy as they walked, and to the left, Agatha could see there was a golf course. To their right, beyond a short expanse of long grass and bracken, was nothing but sea and sky.

"Look!" James's voice was triumphant. He popped the lens cap off his camera. "That's exactly the shot I want." In the distance, the cliffs of the Seven Sisters were shrugging off a veil of mist to bathe in a glory of sunshine, looking

222

impossibly white, the line of the clifftops rising and falling like the back of a ghostly serpent.

James moved off the path towards the cliff edge, searching for the perfect camera angle, and Agatha followed.

"Be careful, my dear," he warned. "Standing too close to the edge is a bad idea. It all gets a bit unstable."

"It's a long way down." Agatha was already peering over the edge and backed away. "Are the cliffs at the Seven Sisters as high as this?"

"Higher," said James. "Go back to the path. I don't want you—"

"Getting hurt?" The voice came from the path, where a bulky figure with a shaven head that seemed to sit on his shoulders with little need for a neck stood facing them.

"Mr. Carver," said Agatha, "we meet at last."

"Just Carver," said the man, stepping forward, trapping Agatha and James between him and the cliff edge. "It's not 'mister.' Carver's not my name. It's just what they call me."

"Why would they call you that if it's not your name?" James asked.

"Because it's what I do," the man answered, reaching behind his back to retrieve from his waistband a large, ugly long-bladed knife. He moved close enough that both Agatha and James were within striking distance.

"Put that down!" James barked. "What do you think you're doing, man?"

"Taking care of you two," came the reply. "That's what I

223

was told to do—and I do as they tell me. I take care of you, or they'll take care of me."

"There's two of us," Agatha pointed out nervously. "You might have that knife, but you're outnumbered."

"He don't worry me much," Carver scoffed, giving James a look of utter derision. He was not quite as tall as James, but he possessed a muscle bulk and an air of menace that made him seem like a giant. "And I'm going to enjoy slicing you up, Mrs. Private Eye. You've really screwed things up for me, and you're going to suffer for it."

"What makes you think I'll let you do that?" Agatha was trembling but defiant.

"Because," Carver gave her an ugly smile, "you can't stop me. You're only a woman."

"Maybe I'm not as weak as you think!" Agatha's voice was a potent mix of fear and anger.

"Oh yeah?" Carver taunted. "What you gonna do? Hit me with your handbag?"

"I could . . ." Agatha offered as her best defence.

"Go on, then." Carver laughed, slapping his free hand against his barrel chest. "Give it your best shot!"

Agatha swung her handbag and hit him not in the chest but in the forehead, the handbag making contact with a sound like a mallet hitting wood. Carver staggered sideways, stunned, blood pouring from a wide gash above his left eye.

"What . . . ?" he mumbled, confused, but Agatha had also moved, sidestepping away from the cliff and delivering another hammer blow from her handbag that landed square on Carver's chin. He groaned and stumbled to his right, dazed, changing places with Agatha and James as if in some bizarre dance ritual.

Carver wiped blood from his eyes to see Agatha, her handbag burst open, haul a house brick from inside it. She stared straight at him and shrugged to let him know that she had never intended to play fair. James snatched the brick from her and hurled it at Carver with all his might. Carver's momentary look of fear turned to a sneer when his free hand caught the brick against his chest, its momentum forcing only a slight backward step. He threw the brick over the cliff and gave his head a shake, clearing his senses to refocus on Agatha and James.

"And that's the best you got?" he sneered, slashing the knife from left to right and lunging forward. As he did so, his feet seemed to lose their grip, and a panicked look shot across his face. There was a brief tearing, scraping sound and the grass beneath his boots sagged, sank and vanished, the cliff edge crumbling beneath him. Arms flailing, he fought to find solid ground, desperately trying to swim through the air, horror widening his eyes. Then he disappeared.

Agatha and James stepped back, away from the cliff. Unable to contain herself, Agatha threw herself flat on the ground and began crawling forward, determined to take a look over the edge. James grabbed her ankles to haul her back, but not before she had peered down on Carver's broken body, splayed and bloodied on the unforgiving rocks far below.

James held her tight and she let out a long sob, the tension and terror bringing tears to her eyes. Then she pulled away from him, looking off towards the Seven Sisters, inland across the golf course and then back along the path to Seaford.

"There's no one else around," she sniffed, accepting a handkerchief that James produced from a pocket. "No one saw a thing."

"No one," James agreed, "and accidents sometimes happen here. People have been known to wander too close to the edge, to fall over and—"

"And," Agatha sprang to her feet, grabbing James's hand, "we have a ferry to catch. Come on, James—I've never felt more like getting lost in France."

Read on for an excerpt from

DEVIL'S DELIGHT—

the next Agatha Raisin novel by
M. C. Beaton and R. W. Green,
coming soon in hardcover
from Minotaur Books!

Chapter One

He was naked.

Some people are easily shocked. Agatha Raisin would never count herself as one of those people. She was a private detective, after all—no wilting flower, no timid swooner, no feeble faintheart. She was made of sterner stuff. Yet even she was a little taken aback. She blinked hard, but when she opened her eyes, he was still there, still naked, in the altogether, not a stitch on, in his birthday suit, in the buff— totally nude. It's not the sort of thing Agatha would normally have expected to see as her assistant was driving her along a quiet country lane and, while not admitting, even to herself, that she was shocked, she was certainly . . . perplexed.

"Agatha . . ." Toni said, slowing the car to a halt, "are you seeing what I'm seeing?"

"If you're seeing a naked young man running down the middle of the road towards us," Agatha replied, unable to tear her eyes away from the spectacle, "then, yes—I'm seeing everything."

The man ran to the driver's side of the car and squatted low, presenting his face, rather than anything else, at the window while knocking urgently on the glass.

"What should I do?" Toni asked, turning to Agatha with a look of panic on her face. "I mean, he could be a carjacker or something. There might be more of them."

"A naked carjacking gang?" Agatha raised her eyebrows. "I think that would be a first. Wind down the window, Toni. Let's hear what he has to say."

"I know it looks a bit strange . . ." said the young man as the window slid down.

"Don't be too hard on yourself," said Agatha. "It all looked perfectly fine to me."

"I mean me not having any clothes on," the young man said quickly, still catching his breath from his dash down the road.

"Let me guess," said Agatha. "A bigger boy stole them and ran away?"

"Please let me explain," he said. "I need your help. I just found a dead body up in those woods!"

Agatha stared at him. His clear green eyes were sharp with fear, and the tremble in his voice came from more than just running.

"Get him something to cover himself up with, Toni," said Agatha. "We need to find out what this is all about."

"Really?" said Toni. "What if he's lying?"

"I've been lied to by many men," Agatha said slowly, "and I pride myself on having learned to tell precisely when a man is lying—especially the naked ones."

"If you say so," Toni said with a sigh, casting around the car for something the young man could use as a cover-up. Her eyes settled on Agatha's hat in the back seat. They were on their way to a wedding—their friends Bill Wong and Alice Peters were tying the knot—and Agatha had agonised over her choice of hat, eventually settling on a deep blue silk skull cap adorned with delicate blue-and-silver silk flowers and surrounded by orbiting swirls of feather-like silk fronds. Toni had gone against Agatha's advice and chosen not to wear a hat.

"No," Agatha said firmly when she saw where Toni was looking. "He's not using my fascinator as some kind of codpiece."

Toni reached under her seat to produce an old, oversized T-shirt that she used for wiping the windscreen.

"Here," she said, passing it out the window. "Maybe you can put your legs through the arms and . . . no . . . everything would drop out of the neck . . ."

"Just cover yourself up,' Agatha said, a sharp note of impatience in her voice, "and get in. I want to see where you found the body. You can tell us how you ended up in this state on the way."

The young man wrapped, tied, and held the T-shirt in place as a makeshift loin cloth, then sat nervously in the back of the car. Toni drove on.

"Start from the beginning," said Agatha. "Tell us who you are and what's happened."

"My name is Edward Carstairs," the young man began. "I'm the social convenor of the Mircester Naturist Club. Take the next turning on the right and you'll come to our clubhouse pavilion."

Toni swung the car across the road and through a gate onto a gravel track that snaked through the dappled shade of tall oak and beech trees, opening out into an area that appeared to be a car park. A red hatchback was parked in front of a single-storey wooden building which, apart from the red-tiled roof, looked like a giant log cabin.

"I came here earlier today to start preparing for our annual barbecue and put our emergency contingency plan in motion," Edward explained.

"Your emergency what?" Toni asked. "What were you all planning?"

"Today's going to be sunny," said Edward. "Tomorrow it's going to rain. I started a phone chain to let people know the barbecue's being brought forward from tomorrow afternoon to this afternoon. I phone two people, they phone two people and so on—all of our members then know within minutes."

"Sounds very efficient," Toni said, "but why not just send an email or text?"

"It's Saturday, so not all of our members will look at an email, and not all of them are comfortable with messaging, but emails and texts were also sent."

"Yes, yes, that all makes perfect sense," Agatha said,

turning to face Edward but finding the sight of him clutching a T-shirt around his groin so awkward that she immediately faced forwards again, "but where does a dead body fit in? And where are your clothes?"

"My clothes are inside," said Edward, "in the male changing room. I'll go grab my shorts and my phone. I need to call the police."

"I think you should let us have a look . . ." Agatha began, but Edward was already out of the car, bounding bare-buttocked up the pavilion steps, having left Toni's T-shirt on the back seat.

"I take it that's not what you wanted us to have a look at," said Toni, watching Edward's naked form disappearing into the building.

"No, I thought it would be a good idea to make sure that someone wasn't playing some kind of practical joke on him before we called the boys in blue."

"Still, he's not difficult to look at, is he?" Toni commented, stepping out of the car, her eyes still on the front door of the building. "I mean—he's fit, good muscle tone, nice tan. Funny little birthmark on his left hip."

"You had a good look, didn't you?" Agatha commented, walking towards the pavilion with Toni.

"We're detectives," Toni said in her defence. "I was using my observational skills."

"So what colour were his eyes?"

"Um . . ."

"Maybe you should have looked at his face, Toni. Then you'd recognise him with his clothes *on*."

231

Agatha pushed open one of the large, glass-panelled oak doors and they entered a spacious, square vestibule. To their right was a door marked WITCHES and to their left one marked WIZARDS. Toni studied the signs with a puzzled expression, but Agatha was more interested in the full-length mirror that took up all of the wall to their left. She smoothed her bob of glossy brown hair, checked her lipstick, and admired the way that her dress was hanging wrinkle-free, even after sitting in the car.

She was extremely proud of the way her dress fitted, having dieted mercilessly and exercised furiously leading up to the wedding in order to achieve the flattest stomach she'd had in years, when she remembered to suck it in a bit. She did so, turning sideways to watch how the open frill that ran from the calf-length hem up to her hip tousled, then settled. Agatha was of the opinion that only women with a good, shapely figure could wear a dress like this. It was off the shoulder but not cut too low, with a tight bodice and a skirt that flared out from the waist.

She glanced at Toni, who was peeking through the door marked WITCHES. She could never get away with this dress. She was beautiful, of course, in that blonde-haired, blue-eyed sort of way, but she was too straight-up-and-down—too skinny. This dress was definitely for the more chic, slightly more mature woman.

"It's off West Carsely Lane," came Edward's voice as he appeared from the WIZARDS door with his phone clamped to his ear and a pair of shorts now covering his magic wand. "Yes, a dead body. I know what I saw! Please hurry!"

"I was hoping you would let us confirm what you'd found before you called the police," Agatha said as Edward rang off. "We have a great deal of experience in these matters and we're on good terms with the local officers. We're actually on our way to the wedding of Detective Sergeant Bill Wong and Detective Constable Alice Peters. I'm Agatha Raisin, private detective and proprietor of Raisin Investigations. This is my colleague, Toni Gilmour."

"Agatha Raisin—yes, of course!" Edward said, recognition dawning on his face. "I've seen you in the Mircester Telegraph. You're the one who caught the gang that was selling endangered animals."

"If you know who I am,' Agatha said, "then you know that it would be a good idea to let us take a look at the body. Lead on."

They followed Edward through an archway opposite the main doors that led into a bar and function area where there was a dance floor around which were arranged tables and chairs. French windows then opened onto a patio extending out to a well-tended lawn bordered by flower beds bursting with the varied, vibrant summer colours of roses, dahlias, and geraniums. To one side of the lawn was a swimming pool and to the other a tennis court.

"I had some time to spare," Edward explained, motioning them to follow him down onto the lawn. Agatha slipped off her high-heeled sandals. She was not fond of walking barefoot, but she knew how easily heels could dig into a lawn. The heels were elegant, but elegance evaporated along with dignity should a heel snap and send you sprawling on your face. "I decided to take a closer look at the Lone Warrior."

"What's the Lone Warrior?" asked Toni.

"It's a huge, ancient stone slab in a clearing in the woods at the far end of our grounds," said Edward. "They say it was once used for human sacrifices. That's where I saw the body. It was sitting on the stone."

"Just sitting there?" said Agatha, wincing slightly when she stepped off the grass onto a vague path at the edge of the woods, where pebbles, twigs, spiky leaves, and other forest-floor debris alien to the tender soles of a city girl's feet lay in ambush. Toni was wearing flat shoes and a look of sympathy. Agatha gritted her teeth and marched on, sandals in one hand, clutch-bag in the other.

"Not actually sitting," said Edward, "more sort of crouching, all hunched over with his face in his hands. It's just through here and . . ."

They walked into a clearing, the sun streaming down between the treetops to create a brightly lit patch on the forest floor. In the middle of the pool of sunlight stood a weathered grey stone. It was three feet tall and six feet long with a flat top wide enough to lie on . . . but nothing lay there. There was no crouched, hunched body on the stone. It sat empty and still in the glade, with only the chattering of chaffinch and blackcap in the treetops subverting the silence.

"It's gone!" Edward gasped, looking around in desperation as he approached the stone. "I swear it was here! You have to believe me!"

"I believe you saw something here," said Agatha, studying the stone, "but in my experience a dead body does not get up and walk away. What exactly did you see here? How close did you get?"

"I saw a man's body, naked, crouching with his face in his hands," Edward replied, continuing to look around as if the body might somehow appear at the base of a tree or in a stand of ferns. "I knew he was dead because the back of his head was all bashed in. There was matted blood in his hair and when I reached out to touch his shoulder, he was stone cold."

"Yet this stone is not cold," Agatha said, laying her hand on the Lone Warrior, "and there's a damp patch in the middle—a little puddle of water."

"Where did that come from?" Toni asked. "It hasn't rained for days."

"It's difficult to make out any footprints amongst all the leaves and weeds," Agatha noted, examining the area around the stone, "but that looks like it might be a tyre track."

"A single tyre track?" Toni said with a frown. "Maybe a motorbike?"

"I didn't hear any motorbike," Edward said. "The thing that spooked me was when I heard a mobile phone ring just as I touched the body. Obviously it wasn't my own phone . . ."

"No pockets," said Toni.

"No trousers," said Agatha.

". . . and I thought that the killers might be lurking in the trees, so I ran," Edward went on. "I ran in that direction." He pointed. "Through the trees, over a fence, and out onto the road."

"Are there any other ways out of here?" Agatha asked.

"I suppose there must be," Edward replied, "but I'm not really sure. I've only been down here a couple of times, and I've always gone back to the pavilion from here."

"There are various paths through the woods," said Toni, studying her phone, on which she had called up an aerial view of the area. "They appear to lead to tracks that run down to the road we were on as well as a couple of other minor roads heading in the direction of Mircester."

"So, anyone hiding in the woods watching you," Agatha pondered, scanning the tree line all around the clearing, "could have made off without returning to the pavilion and without us seeing them."

"But if someone had decided to dump a body here," Toni said, frowning, "why would they then take it away again?"

"Maybe they didn't want to dump it here," said Agatha, still peering into the woods. "Maybe they were disturbed by nudie Eddie and hid until he was gone. Then they moved the body to somewhere like—over there where there are thick shrubs under the trees." Agatha pointed to the spot. "That looks like a—"

"Nice place to dump a body" said Toni, then, returning Agatha's and Edward's bemused stares with a shrug, added, "She says it all the time."

"I do *not* say it all the time," argued Agatha.

"Yes, you do," said Toni. "Every time we pass a—"

"Just go take a look." Agatha cut Toni short, then lifted one foot to display immaculately painted toenails. "I had a pedicure yesterday. It's survived this far, but I'm not ruining it scuffling around over there."

Toni and Edward picked their way through the tangle of ferns and brambles to where a clutch of tall rhododendrons stood in the shade of the trees. Toni picked up a stick to prod around in the undergrowth, shining a light from her phone to illuminate the darkest recesses of the dense shrubbery.

"There's nothing there, Agatha," she called, looking back towards the Lone Warrior, on which Agatha had now parked her sandals, then pointing beyond her boss, through the trees towards the swimming pool, "but here comes trouble!"

Agatha turned, catching a glimpse of the unmistakable form of Detective Chief Inspector Wilkes marching down the lawn. He was wearing a suit that was somewhere between brown and grey, matching his greying hair and pallid complexion. It occurred to Agatha that, if he were to lie down on the forest floor, no one would ever notice him. He would merge right into the decaying debris of sticks and fallen leaves and probably never be seen again. Unfortunately, however, she could see him quite clearly now. He was a tall, thin man and, even on this gloriously sunny day, appeared darkly miserable. His beady eyes glowered from beneath a furrowed brow when he spotted Agatha.

"What are you doing here?" he barked.

"Same as you," said Agatha. "Looking for a corpse."

"This is a police matter," he said, glancing over his

shoulder to where two uniformed officers were jogging past the swimming pool towards him. He waved at them to hurry. "One of my officers will take a statement from you, then you can be on your way."

"A statement about what?" Agatha asked. "I can't see that any crime's been committed."

"That's for me to decide, not you," Wilkes said curtly. "Where is the person who reported finding a body?"

"The young man over there in the shorts," Agatha said, pointing to Edward, who was picking his way back through the brambles with Toni, "but the body he found seems to have gone missing."

"What are you talking about, woman?" Wilkes snapped. "How can a body disappear?"

"I understand it was sitting on this stone slab," Agatha explained, stooping to examine the surface of the stone, "but by the time we got here, there was only a little puddle of water. Even that's dried up now."

"Ridiculous!" Wilkes barked. "Bodies do not simply evaporate like water!"

"I know what I saw," said Edward. "There was the body of a man with his head all bashed in. I was startled by a phone ringing in the bushes and ran off to find help."

"You need to cordon off the area and get some forensics people out here," said Agatha. "There will have to be a fingertip search of the surrounding woodland and—"

"There will be no such thing!" Wilkes said, a sweep of his hand drawing a line under the idea. "Do not try to tell me my job, Mrs. Raisin."

"As we've seen so often in the past, Chief Inspector," Agatha said, setting her chin and folding her arms, "apparently someone has to."

"I don't have the manpower to waste on what is clearly some kind of practical joke," Wilkes said bluntly. "Half the force seems to have taken leave in order to attend the wedding of DS Wong and DC Peters."

"I take it you weren't invited?" Agatha gave Wilkes a transparently insincere smile and picked up her sandals. "Toni and I are on our way there now."

"It's a lovely day for a wedding," came a low, powerful voice from the direction of the pavilion.

Agatha and Wilkes turned to see a dark-haired man approaching. Agatha judged him to be in his mid to late forties. He was not quite as tall as Wilkes but was more powerfully built, with broad shoulders and well-defined muscles. He had piercing blue eyes, tanned skin, and a beard styled and clipped with bonsai precision. The hair on the rest of his body was equally well-groomed, artfully trimmed to show off his impressive physique to best advantage. Agatha was able to assess his physical attributes so thoroughly because, like Edward when he had come running down the lane, the newcomer was entirely naked. Unlike young Edward, the bearded man had an aura of calm maturity, radiating confidence in a way that Agatha found beguilingly attractive, despite his beard. Agatha had never liked beards. She had a sudden urge to check her lipstick but settled instead for a little extra abdominal squeeze to hold her tummy taught.

"What do you think you're playing at, man?" Wilkes bellowed. "Put some clothes on at once!"

"I don't feel inclined to dress myself right now," answered the man.

"You don't feel . . . ? Gittins!" Wilkes yelled at one of the uniformed constables, frantically beckoning him closer. "Arrest that man!"

"Er . . . what am I nicking him for, sir?" asked the constable.

"He's to be charged under section sixty-six, Sexual Offences Act 2003—exposing his genitals intending to cause alarm or distress," Wilkes stiffly quoted the regulations.

"Are you going to arrest all of them, too?" asked Agatha, nodding towards the lawn, where a small crowd of naked men and women of all ages, shapes, and sizes was beginning to gather, standing and staring like a throng of fleshy statues. When he spotted the undressed horde, Wilkes's mouth dropped open.

"The thing is, sir," said Constable Gittins, "this here's a naturist club, so everyone's allowed to go around in the altogether."

"Thanks for explaining, Ian," said the bearded man, giving the constable a nod of gratitude.

"You know this man, Gittins?" Wilkes said, frowning at his junior officer.

"Oh, yes, sir," said Gittins. "Everyone knows Jasper Crane. He's our chairman."

"OUR chairman?" Wilkes was flabbergasted. "You mean you're—"

240

"Exactly, Chief Inspector," Jasper said with a smile. "Ian is one of our members. Will we be seeing you for the barbecue later, Ian?"

"Me and the missus will be here soon as I finish me shift," said Gittins, removing his cap to fan himself while tugging at his bulky, stab-proof utility vest to let some air circulate. "Can't wait for a dip in the pool."

"Well," Wilkes muttered, "I'm glad I won't be here to witness that." Then he raised his voice to talk to Gittins. "Disperse that crowd of . . . your friends up there, Gittins, and you," he pointed to the other constable, "have a good look around for anything suspicious, then take a statement from the person who phoned this in. I'm going back to the office."

"Is that it?" asked Agatha. "You're not going to launch a proper enquiry?"

"Whatever your friend in the shorts saw," said Wilkes, "always assuming he hasn't completely lost his marbles and was hallucinating, was undoubtedly a prank played on him by his nudist chums. If I need any sort of statement from you, Mrs. Raisin, I always know where to find you. I just have to look for trouble and you're never far away."

"And you're even easier to find," Agatha replied, fixing Wilkes with her bear-like eyes. "All I have to do is turn over the nearest rock and out you crawl."

Wilkes gave a "harrumph" and marched off towards the pavilion, breezing past two petite, middle-aged women. Each of the women was wearing a loose-fitting caftan embroidered with gold astrological symbols. They made for Jasper, one of them offering him a black silk robe.

"We thought you might want this while you talked to the prudes," she said.

"Thank you, ladies," said Jasper, treating them to a warm smile and shrugging on the robe. It was decorated with gold images of fiery suns, glowing planets, twinkling stars, and streaking comets. There were no fastenings but the edges met in the middle, covering his nakedness. The women bowed and walked back the way they had come, flinging off their caftans when they reached the lawn.

"Prudes?" Agatha enquired with a raised eyebrow.

"It's just a little fun term we use when we have clothed visitors at the club." Jasper laughed. "We refer to ourselves as the 'nudes' and clothed people as 'prudes'—too prudish to disrobe, you see."

"Yes, I do see," said Agatha, bristling slightly. "I don't think I've ever been called "prudish" before."

"Please don't be insulted. You and your friend are more than welcome to join us here any time you like." He swept his left arm towards the clubhouse. The robe had openings for his arms but no sleeves, the silk drifting up to his elbow and wafting open down the middle, allowing Agatha another glimpse of what had previously been covered. In an instant, she realised she was staring and averted her eyes.

"It's all right to look," he said gently. "We all look, we all compare—that's human nature and we are, after all, naturists. What we don't do is judge."

"How very . . . reassuring," Agatha said.

"Agatha, we really need to get going," said Toni, looking at her watch.

"Ah, yes . . . the wedding," Jasper said. "Allow me to walk you to the pavilion."

"I'd like to have a quick word with Edward first," Agatha said, and joined him and Toni on the other side of the Lone Warrior.

"I'm really sorry about all of this, Mrs. Raisin," Edward said, "but I honestly saw a body sitting right here on the stone. I wasn't making it up. Now I feel like I've wasted your time."

"I don't like people playing tricks on me," Agatha said tersely, "and if that's what you were doing, I'll make sure you regret it."

Edward looked down at the ground, shuffling his feet like a naughty schoolboy in front of the headmistress.

"But I don't think that's what happened here," Agatha went on. "I think you were telling the truth, yet there doesn't appear to be any evidence of a crime—certainly not a brutal murder. It's a mystery and I hate leaving things unresolved."

"We'll help you find out what it's all about, won't we, Agatha?" Toni offered eagerly. "We'll help you get to the bottom of it, Edward."

"Well . . . yes, of course," Agatha agreed, slightly taken aback by Toni's unbridled enthusiasm. "When the officer takes your statement, be sure to ask for a copy. We can at least go over it all together at some point."

Edward thanked them for being so understanding, then

he and Toni followed as Jasper escorted Agatha back to the pavilion. Even more people had now arrived, turning the garden and pool area into a hive of activity. Keen gardeners wearing nothing more than sturdy gloves were deadheading the roses, the perimeter hedge was being clipped, bugs and leaves were being fished out of the pool, and the patio was being swept. Agatha had never seen so many naked people. They smiled and waved as she walked by, making her feel completely welcome and yet utterly out of place at the same time.